MAX

MI c

Please return or renew this item before the latest date shown below

9/22

East Mobile

1 6 MAY 2023

Renewals can be made
by internet   www.onfife.com/fife-libraries
in person   at any library in Fife
by phone   03451 55 00 66

AT FIFE

Thank you for using your libı

D1420017

For all students and staff at Wenlock Junior School.
We are all Team Wenlock.

First published in the UK in 2022 by Nosy Crow Ltd
The Crow's Nest, 14 Baden Place
Crosby Row, London, SE1 1YW, UK

Nosy Crow Eireann Ltd
44 Orchard Grove, Kenmare
Co Kerry, V93 FY22, Ireland

www.nosycrow.com

ISBN: 978 1 83994 730 8

Nosy Crow and associated logos are trademarks and/or registered
trademarks of Nosy Crow Ltd

Text copyright © Jeremy Williams, 2022
Cover illustration copyright © Thy Bui, 2022

A CIP catalogue record for this book is available from the
British Library.

Printed and bound in the UK by Clays Ltd, Elcograf S.p.A.
Typeset by Tiger Media

Papers used by Nosy Crow are made from wood grown in
sustainable forests

1 3 5 7 9 10 8 6 4 2

1

When people hear that my name is Max and that I counted to a million, they always say "Maximillian! How appropriate!" I've heard SO MANY adults say that. All of them said it as if they were the first to think of it. But my name isn't Maximillian, or Maximus, or Maxwell, or any other random thing that you could shorten to Max.

It's just Max.

That is what it says on my birth certificate.

I've seen my birth certificate. My mum showed it to me once when she was looking for something. It's an important

piece of paper that the government writes when you're born. It's to say that you officially exist. My name also appears on other things, like the sign on my bedroom door or written on the inside of my coat. Those are not official and have nothing to do with the government.

On my birth certificate it says that my name is Max Cromwell and that I was born in 2011. I was eight years old when I started counting to a million, and nine when I finished, and that's why I got the world record for being the youngest person to do it.

You might have just shouted "spoiler alert!" in your head. But the book is called *Max Counts to a Million*, so it's a bit late for that.

Not many people have counted to a million in real life. I have, and so I can tell you it's not easy. It took me weeks. I'm quite proud of it, though there are bits of my story that I'm not so proud of. I've decided I'm going to put those bits in too, so that it's all true.

All of this happened in 2020. As you probably know, that was a very strange year. It's when the coronavirus came along and everything went very weird. We weren't even allowed to leave our houses, and that's why I started counting. But that's jumping ahead.

Let me start at the beginning.

· ○ ★ ○ ·

It was an ordinary day. Let's say it was a Tuesday.

Tuesdays are usually the worst day of the week. That's a fact. I know people say Mondays are the worst, but at least it's the start of a new week. You're fresh out of a weekend and ready to go. Wednesdays are the middle of the week, and on Wednesdays I like to look at the clock at midday and see the week go past halfway. Thursdays are OK because the next day is Friday, and then Friday is Friday. So Tuesday is definitely the most boring and ordinary day.

For that reason, it was a Tuesday.

I was at school – an ordinary school. This

isn't going to be one of those stories set in a boarding school or a wizarding school or anything. It was a normal day, with lessons and lunch and more lessons and the usual stuff. Mum picked me up in the afternoon, and that's when it started to get less ordinary.

She was worried about something. I could tell. She waved to me across the playground and said hello, and asked how my day had gone and gave me a sort of side-hug. But I knew two things straightaway. One: she was worried. Two: she didn't want me to know she was worried.

You might be wondering how I knew this, when I was only eight and not even a detective. There were a few reasons. One was the side-hug. That's not something mums do. Side-hugs are for uncles who don't have children of their own yet and don't know how to hug a person who is smaller than they are. Mums always hug properly, and so I knew something was up.

I also knew something was wrong because when Mum asked what I had for lunch, I said "fish finger pie", and she said, "OK, that's nice." Fish finger pie is not a thing and it must never be allowed to exist. Something was clearly on her mind.

"Have you had a good day, Mum?" I asked, and she made a sort of "hmm" noise that wasn't even an answer. It was as if she hadn't heard me. I decided I'd better hold her hand on the walk home, in case she wandered into a road.

2

My birth certificate lives in a drawer of Very Important Papers in my parents' room. My passport is in there too. I'm not allowed to touch that drawer, but it's good to know it's there. Just in case I have to flee the country in a hurry. Or if I need to quickly check that I exist.

This bit about birth certificates is a good example of a tangent.

That's when you're talking about something, and you accidentally start talking about something else. I showed my mum the first chapter of my story and she said I need to be careful of them.

I'd better get back to the story.

Usually my dad gets home a bit after I've had my dinner. Mum keeps his dinner in the microwave and he heats it up, and we talk while he eats and I load the dishwasher. That's the deal. Mum cooks, and I do the dishwasher. But today Dad was late. I was already in my pyjamas when he came home, and he sat at the table looking very tired.

I noticed that he hadn't finished his food. Dad always finishes his food.

"Max, has anyone at school mentioned the coronavirus?" he asked.

"The what?"

"The coronavirus. Maybe in assembly or something?"

I thought about it. I might have heard that word in assembly that day. Did Ms Ryba, the deputy head, mention it? She stood up to make an announcement, and that might have been a word that she said. I didn't really hear her, because I was looking around to see who was behind me and kicking me in the back. It was Miles. Then I was whispering at him to stop. Then I was trying to wipe the dusty marks off my blazer. By the time I had finished, Ms Ryba was sitting down again.

"No?" said Dad, while I was still thinking about it. "Let me know if it comes up at school, OK? And remember to wash your hands before you eat anything."

Adults ask if you know about all kinds of things, like cuboids, the equator, or Shakespeare, and they're always telling you to wash your hands. So Dad's questions didn't seem all that strange right then. I was going to ask him what it was all about, but Mum was calling me to brush my teeth.

My dad is a doctor. He works at the hospital. A lot of doctors focus on one part of the body, and he focuses on people's ears, noses and throats. There's a fancy name for that kind of doctor, but I can't remember it and I definitely can't spell it.

If you've got a problem with your ears, nose or throat, my dad is the person to see. For example, sometimes children stick things up their noses, like peas or Lego.

Do not do this. It's a very bad idea.

This is not what noses are for.

Still, it happens, usually to very small children. And when it does, my dad is the one who has to get out a tiny torch and shine it up their nostril.

Or maybe you've gone swimming and got water in your ear. Sometimes it gets stuck, and then you can't hear properly. Dad's got another little torch that can look right down inside your ear and he'll sort you out.

Those are easy things for an expert. If Dad is late home from work, it means that something more serious is going on. But I didn't get to find out about it because it was already bedtime.

9

At least, my parents didn't plan for me to find out about it.

· ∘ ★ ∘ ·

When I was in bed, my parents went back downstairs. I was all set to go to sleep, and then I remembered that I had left my emergency glass of water in the bathroom. I got up quietly to go and get it. As I tiptoed past the top of the stairs, I heard Mum and Dad talking.

Grown-ups always do their most serious talking when their children have just gone to bed. It's like they've been waiting all day to tell each other really important adult things. I've practised my spying skills to listen to them a few times. I hoped I would hear something juicy, like what they're planning to get me for my birthday, but it's always really boring. Stuff about bills, or filling in a form. I don't know what it is exactly, but there's this thing called insurance that seems to make Dad angry.

Since they'd both been a bit weird that day, I

paused to listen.

"So it's happening then, is it?" Mum was saying.

"It's happening," said Dad. He was pacing up and down in the kitchen. "No confirmed cases locally yet, but it's only a matter of time."

"But that's not your department," said Mum.

"It's everyone's department if it goes the way it has elsewhere. It's all hands on deck."

"In the wards?"

"I'm afraid so."

They were complaining about Dad's work by the sound of it. Grumbling about their jobs was a regular subject in those after-bedtime chats, so I went and got my water from the bathroom. On the way back, I heard something else.

"What about the schools?" Mum asked. "How long can they stay open?"

Obviously that caught my attention. I stopped and sat down on the top step, sipping my water.

"Ireland have already called it. France. Spain.

11

It's not long until the holidays. I think the government are hoping to hold on until then and see how it goes."

Talking about the government was another popular topic for this time of day, but this was different. Were they seriously talking about closing schools? This should have been happier news, except that Mum and Dad were obviously worried. Scared, even. I didn't like that. What was going on? Should I be worried?

I listened a few minutes longer. None of it made much sense, and I couldn't hear everything as they rattled about in the kitchen. But then I did catch one more bit.

"What do we tell Max?" said Dad.

"Nothing. There's no need to worry him just yet."

So, yes. Apparently I should be worried.

3

On Wednesdays I have football before school. This is one of the reasons I like Wednesdays, as well as watching the clock go past halfway at lunchtime. Unfortunately, it means getting me to school at seven forty-five, which is basically the world's earliest time. So there's a lot of whining involved.

"Haven't you finished your breakfast yet? Why haven't you got your shoes on?"

Dad looks down and realises he is leaving the house in his slippers.

"Look, you've got toast crumbs all over yourself. And are you sure you're going to be warm enough in that? You should put something long-sleeved on."

Dad brushes the crumbs off his T-shirt, puts his hoody on and we finally get on our way.

Honestly, leaving the house is such a battle sometimes.

This particular day was a good one, because I scored a hat-trick in football. Miles was in goal as well – the boy who was kicking me in assembly. When I scored, he was the one who had to pick the ball out of the net. Ha.

A hat-trick is a strange name for scoring three goals. I asked Mr Collins the PE teacher why it's called that. He said that the first person to get a hat-trick was in cricket, when a bowler got three wickets in three balls. His friends celebrated by buying him a new top hat. I asked Mr Collins if he could get me a top hat for scoring three goals, but he said no.

If we still gave people top hats for scoring

hat-tricks, I would have three top hats right now. That would be kind of pointless, since nobody wears top hats any more. And I don't have three heads.

It would be useful if I was learning to be a magician though. I could learn hat tricks with my hat-trick hats.

This is definitely a tangent.

At school that day, I made sure to listen out for the corona thing that Dad had asked about. I was also watching the teachers. Were they being weird too?

I mean, more weird than usual. There are a couple of teachers who are always weird. Like Miss Jenkins, one of the other teachers in Year Four, who tucks the end of one of her trouser legs into her sock. Why?

It wasn't that kind of odd that I was looking out for though. It was the shifty behaviour, the whispers. The way the grown-ups were worried and pretending they weren't.

Sure enough, I saw it for myself pretty quickly. I volunteered to take the register down to the office. The office ladies were all talking when I came in, and as soon as I knocked on the door they stopped and looked at me. They're usually friendly and quite used to people coming and going. They were obviously talking about something the children weren't supposed to hear.

Probably the corona thing.

"Mustn't worry the children," they were probably thinking. I wanted to tell them how pointless this was. What's more worrying: knowing about something serious, or knowing that there's something serious going on that nobody is talking about? At least if you know what it is, then you can decide for yourself whether it's scary or not.

Anyway, I don't think I need to be protected from serious things. I'm not little any more. I watch the news with my dad sometimes. I know that bad things happen in the world. I'm not scared. I'm not going to freak out.

Unless the country is being invaded by giant spiders. Then I certainly will FREAK OUT.

But that's not what's happening. I know we're not being invaded by giant spiders, because they don't exist except in Australia.

And there's no way my parents would have been talking calmly about it last night, either. If giant spiders were on the way, Mum would be cramming everything she owns into a suitcase. She'd be grabbing our passports from the drawer of Very Important Papers and screaming about moving to Canada. Dad would be in the kitchen, working out how to make a spider-catching device out of the wheelie bin.

I wondered if any of the other children knew what was going on. At playtime I asked Felix. Felix is a good friend, and not just because he has an X in his name and he is part of Team X.

"Do you know what's going on with everyone at the moment?" I asked him while we were taking turns trying to stand on a tennis ball. "All the grown-ups and the corona thing?"

"Oh, the coronavirus," said Felix. "Yeah, it sounds pretty bad. My mum said that it's a new kind of virus."

"So it makes you sick?"

"It's like a cold but times a thousand. It gives you a really bad cough. And I heard it makes you lose your taste – like everything just tastes of nothing."

"That's weird," I said.

"Yeah, well, tons of people have got it."

This didn't sound good.

"Have people at school got it?"

"No, but they might have to close the school. Mum says it's very infectious, which means it's super easy to catch. So if one person in a class gets it, then everyone else might get it too."

I took my turn on the tennis ball, which must

18

have been left behind from PE.

I tried to remember. There had been some stuff on the news about a virus. The other day they had shown pictures from a hospital that was too full of sick people. I didn't know where it was, and I didn't really understand it because I was trying to fix my Lego space shuttle at the time. I had accidentally thrown it across the room during blast-off.

I know it sounds like I'm really bad at paying attention. School assembly and the news had both mentioned coronavirus and I still hadn't heard it properly. But I've already told you that Miles was kicking me in assembly. And I was dealing with quite a serious crash when the news was on. Some of the pieces of the shuttle had flown all the way behind the sofa. The pilot was lucky to survive.

I made a note to talk to Dad more about it when I got home. Felix was about to say something else, but we were rudely interrupted by Mrs

19

Malik rushing towards us across the playground.

"Are you standing on that ball?" she demanded, arms flapping in alarm. "Don't stand on balls. You'll break your neck."

4

That week I learned a new word: pandemic. I had seen the word before because my parents have a board game called Pandemic. It's a grown-up board game that they play with friends after I've gone to bed, so I don't know what happens in it. Since it had "pan" in the name, I thought it was a cooking game. Like maybe you're a chef in a restaurant and loads of people are ordering food, and you have to cook the right things. I think you could make a good board game about that. It would have to be an adult board game because chefs like to swear a lot.

So when Dad asked me that night if I knew what a pandemic was, I said, "Yes. It's when everything goes wrong in the kitchen."

Dad laughed because he thought I was making a joke. Then he saw that I wasn't, and he quickly stopped so that I wouldn't feel bad. He was too late and I felt a bit silly.

A pandemic is when an illness spreads everywhere in the world. Dad said that when a word has "pan" at the beginning it means all of something, or everything. He said a few long words beginning with "pan" as examples. They sounded medical and complicated. I must have looked confused, because he tried again.

"OK... Pantheist. That's someone who believes that God is in everything. Panacea. That's a cure for everything."

I still looked at him without saying anything.

"Panorama – a view of everything."

I'd heard of that one.

"Oh, I get it," I said. "What about pants?"

"No, that's not one of them."

"Pancake?"

"Not that one either."

"Panda?"

Dad shook his head.

In other words, sometimes "pan" at the beginning of the word means "everything". Sometimes it doesn't. The people in charge of the English language need to make up their minds.

A pandemic is very rare, which is lucky. There was a famous one about a hundred years ago, when there was a kind of flu that went around the world. Coronavirus was a new one. It was a virus that was hopping from country to country as people travelled on planes. Now it had landed in Britain, and all the doctors in the country were getting ready.

Dad and I were sitting at the kitchen table. He had finished his dinner and I was drinking a glass of milk. Mum was on the phone to

Grandma (that's her mum). Because Dad is a doctor, he knows all about every kind of medical emergency. I had decided to ask him for all the details about the coronavirus. Then I'd be able to explain it to the teachers if they were worried.

"Let me get this straight," I said to Dad. "The coronavirus is getting on a plane?"

"Not exactly. The people travel on planes. The virus travels in the people."

"It rides around in people?"

"Basically. You know that time we went to the Science Museum in London?"

I nodded extra hard because I remembered that day very well.

"We had to get off one train and get on to another one. That's what a virus does. It's always moving. It has to get off one person and on to another one, all the time. And it does that by travelling through the air when people cough, and then being breathed in by someone else. Which is a problem, because it also makes people cough a lot."

So now there are planes and trains involved, and the coronavirus travelling about with a tiny suitcase.

A suitcase full of coughs to give people.

I nodded again to show that I understood, even though I didn't.

"I don't understand why the coronavirus wants to make people sick," I said.

"Well…" Dad began. He paused and dipped his finger in some leftover sauce on his plate and licked it. He's told me off for doing that before, but he seemed to have forgotten.

"A virus doesn't really want to make people sick. It doesn't want anything. It doesn't make choices. It's not even really alive – not the way we understand being alive."

This didn't make any sense at all.

The only thing I could think of that wasn't really alive was zombies. Now I was imagining tiny zombies with suitcases, flying out of somebody's

mouth when they coughed and coming down on parachutes.

"A virus isn't really a living thing, but it's not dead either," Dad explained. "It's like a rogue bit of computer code. All it can do is make more of itself and move on. It's like a glitch."

I understood what a glitch was. Once I built an amazing castle in Minecraft. Then there was a glitch when it was saving, and it all disappeared. Glitches could ruin everything.

"Look, there's a lot to take in," said Dad. "It's new for all of us. The virus was only discovered at the end of last year, which is why the illness that you get from it is called Covid-19 – short for Coronavirus Disease 2019. Scientists and doctors are working round the clock all over the world to find out what the virus does, but we're having to work it out as we go along. Just remember to wash your hands. And the most important thing is that you don't need to worry."

That again. Everybody working hard to make

sure the children weren't worried. But how was that possible? Here was a very dangerous, very rare and very complicated thing that even doctors were trying to understand. And the only thing that children needed to know about it was that they shouldn't worry.

Anyway, I had learned the word pandemic. It's the kind of word that's a bit sad to learn. If you're lucky, it's a word you never need to use, or know the meaning of, or even know exists. There are quite a lot of words like that. Like vomit, or politics, or courgette.

The longer you can go without knowing about these things, the happier your life will be. That is a fact.

5

I realise that we have got all the way to chapter five of this book about counting to a million, and I haven't even started yet.

We'll get there, don't worry. This stuff before I start counting is all part of the story.

· · ★ · ·

We made it to the weekend, and on Saturday mornings I usually go shopping with Mum. I haven't told you much about my mum yet. I've put more about my dad at the beginning of the book because — well, you'll see why in a bit.

Where to start with my mum?

My mum is called Em, but if you're thinking M for Max, that's not right. It's Em short for Emily, and her name begins with an E. The most important thing to say about my mum is that she is amazing and I love her very much. I'm not just putting that in because she'll read this later. It's true even on the days when I forget.

But we are a bit different.

I'm not a loud and annoying person. At least, I don't think so. But I do like to chat, and I like to be around people. So does my dad. If he is looking after me for the day, we spend the whole time together. We talk about everything.

Mum is a bit quieter than me and Dad. Her volume dial is just set lower. She's not shy, and she can be rowdy and silly as well sometimes. Just not as often. When it's just me and Mum around the house, I'll usually end up playing by myself in my room for a bit. We'll sit quietly and do some reading. Everybody needs their own space sometimes, and Mum needs it more often than I do – some alone time to recharge her batteries.

Saturday mornings are not Mum's alone time. That's when we go shopping together. Mum is in charge of the list. I'm in charge of pushing the trolley.

I like pushing the trolley. I'm not allowed to try driving the car yet, even when there's not much traffic. The trolley is as close as I get to driving something. But I do occasionally wish that we could swap jobs: Mum could push the trolley and I'd be in charge of the shopping list.

This is another thing about Mum. She has a particular job that affects how she writes a shopping list. She thinks it makes her better at it. I think it makes her worse. You see, my mum is a nutritionist.

A nutritionist is someone who knows all about healthy food. Mum's job is to help people to make better choices about what they eat. She's obsessed with people getting their five portions a day of fruit and vegetables – *at least* five portions, as Mum always adds. When we're in the shops, she often stops to read the ingredients on a packet, and then huffs and puts it back on the shelf.

Usually these are foods that I asked for, and this is why I'd like to be in charge of the shopping list for a change. Parents should really think about the way that their careers will affect their children.

We got to the shops, and we soon found out that school was not the only thing that had gone strange that week. The supermarket had gone weird too.

We felt it the moment we walked in the door. Something was not right. All the shoppers seemed nervous. The people coming out, with their trolleys piled high, looked stressed and unhappy. And we soon saw why.

Something had gone wrong in supermarket world. It was half empty.

We were in the fresh fruit and vegetable section. Mum's favourite bit. The shelves were bare – just piles of empty green plastic crates. Mum looked at her list and then at the shelves, and her arm dropped to her side. Her mouth dropped open. No words came out.

I looked along the vegetable display. One box had some onion skins in it, the brown flaky bits that slip off when you pick up an onion. No actual onions. Another had some white and green stems. Perhaps the bits that you tear off a cauliflower. No actual cauliflower.

I smiled.

I don't hate vegetables. I would not survive in my house if I hated vegetables. But I don't get excited about them either. I like the brightly coloured ones: sweetcorn, carrots, tomatoes. The green ones I'm not too fussed about, but I will eat them if I have to. Even sprouts. I like to pretend that I'm a giant and I'm eating a whole cabbage in one bite. As long as I focus on

32

pretending I'm a big farty giant, I don't notice the taste.

We all have to draw the line somewhere, and I draw it at courgette. It is the cucumber's evil twin and should not be trusted.

But there was no danger of courgettes today. Even they had all gone.

Mum was obviously more upset about this than I was.

"Shall we see what else is on the list?" I said cheerfully. I hoped it was cheerful enough to make her feel better, but not so cheerful that she'd realise I was happy about the shortage of vegetables.

I pushed the trolley down towards the fridge aisles and felt the sudden cold on my legs. Every week I feel that shudder and remind myself not to wear my football shorts to the supermarket next time. And every week I forget again. But we didn't need to stay long here either. The meat was all gone, the yoghurt, the milk. The

33

only thing left in the dairy section was some sheep's cheese and a kind of mouldy blue monster cheese called Gorgonzola.

Did this have to do with the coronavirus too? Had the tiny zombies run off with everything?

Mum finally spoke.

"I had heard about this. I didn't realise it was this bad."

It was the "Panic Buying", she explained. When people think a shop is going to run out of something, they hurry there and buy as much as they can. And then, because too many people bought too much of something all at once, it does run out.

So the thing that people were afraid of happens because people were afraid of it. The shelves were empty because people were afraid that there would be empty shelves.

The further we walked into the shop, the further my smile sank. No vegetables was something I could live with, but when we got to the pasta aisle, that was a different matter. If we had no fresh food or if Mum was in a hurry, she'd do pasta and sauce. Those were happy days for me. But today the supermarket had no pasta and no sauce.

There was just nothing there. You could see right to the metal at the back of the shelves.

"This is… This is…" said Mum as we stood in the aisle. I didn't know what she thought it was.

Others had more to say. A man was talking angrily to someone in a supermarket uniform, who was shrugging and saying sorry. Apparently there was a shortage of toilet paper, and he was NOT happy about it. Some shoppers were rushing from aisle to aisle, grabbing whatever foods were left on the shelves. Others just looked dazed. It was all too strange to take in and they drifted along in silence.

An older man walked by with a shopping basket over his arm. He had a jar of Marmite and a packet of ready-made pancakes in it, and that was all. I imagined him going home and eating them together. Marmite pancakes.

Pandemic pancakes.

Panicakes.

Pan for everything.

Everything gone strange.

6

The supermarket trip wasn't a complete disaster. People had bought all the fresh fruit and vegetables, and all the tinned ones. They seemed to have forgotten about the frozen fruit and veg, so we loaded up with sweetcorn and green beans, ice cream, frozen berries and mango.

"I hope there's room for it all," mumbled Mum. "Is there anywhere in the house that we could fit a second freezer?"

"Are you about to panic-buy a freezer?" I asked.

We didn't talk any more about another freezer.

Instead, Mum looked at all the frozen stuff in the trolley and decided what was most important. The ice cream went back on the shelf, and Mum replaced it with another bag of frozen peas.

I should have let her panic-buy the freezer.

Still, on the way out we had to queue past the mini-shelf that supermarkets put by the checkout. There's always chewing gum and sweets, and little packets of tissues. Last-minute things to tempt people to spend a tiny bit more money after they thought they had everything they wanted.

"I see there are still Smarties in the world," I said.

I didn't actually ask for them, you'll notice. I just pointed them out. As Mum is a nutritionist there is absolutely no point in asking her for sweets. But just this once, Mum smiled at me and put a tube on to the checkout conveyor belt.

"That's to make up for putting the ice cream back."

· ∘ ★ ∘ ·

On the way home there was a bit of a traffic jam. It was as if everybody in the world had decided they needed to go to the supermarket RIGHT NOW. Mum drummed her fingers on the steering wheel and put on the radio.

"Is it OK if I open my Smarties?" I asked.

"Sure," Mum replied, looking at me in the rear-view mirror.

It was a question I had thought about. If I'd asked, "Can I eat my Smarties?" Mum would have said, "Yes, but not all at once." But I'd asked if I could *open* my Smarties, which was much more innocent. She had given no instructions on how many I could eat, and so I planned to eat them all.

Because I have no brothers and sisters, I have the whole back of the car to myself. The back of the middle seat folds down into an armrest

with cup-holders in it. I pulled it down and carefully poured the Smarties into the cup-holder. Then I picked them back out again, one at a time. I sorted them and lined them up on the armrest in order of least to most favourite: pink ones first, then purple. Then brown, yellow, red, green, orange, blue.

Not many people know this, but orange Smarties are the only one with a flavour. They taste a tiny bit like orange. If you think the other colours taste different from each other, it's just in your head.

First of all, I scooped up all the pink ones and leaned forwards.

"These are for you," I said to Mum.

"Thank you, that's very kind," she replied.

It was.

It was also clever. If somebody buys you chocolate and you share it with them, they are more likely to buy you chocolate again. Probably about twice as likely. So even though you give some away, you get more in total.

You could do some real-life maths with this if you wanted to:

Chocolate without sharing: one whole tube of Smarties to yourself.

Chocolate with sharing: one tube, minus some for Mum, equals second tube of Smarties.

No, hang on.

The pink Smarties are one of the eight colours, so that's an eighth. With seven eighths left for me.

7/8 + 7/8 = 14/8

14 divided by 8 is 1, remainder 6.

I should not have bothered with this.

No, wait.

OK, I've got it. If I share the tube and Mum buys me another one soon, and I share that one too, then I get one and three quarters in total.

Boom.

That is scientific proof that it is better to share chocolate. Just a little bit.

· · ★ · ·

Not everyone eats Smarties the way I do. You might have your own order for the colours, and that's fine. But don't do what my dad does.

He bought some for me once. "Can I have a couple?" he asked, without waiting for me to offer. And then before I had answered, he just poured some into his hand. He didn't count them, so even though he'd specifically asked for *a couple*, it was more than two. Had he forgotten that a couple means two? Or did he ask for less than he planned to take – just to make sure I'd say yes?

Anyway, then he just flipped his hand up and ate them all in one mouthful, all mixed together. I found this very disrespectful.

Disrespectful to me, and to the Smarties.

Eating things all in one handful is fine when they are all the same, like raisins. Or when things are meant to be mixed together, like nuts and raisins. If somebody has gone to the trouble of making sweets different colours, surely they're supposed to be eaten separately. There are other chocolates that all look the same, like Maltesers or Buttons. Buy those instead if you're going to scoff them by the handful!

• • ★ • •

I might have talked too much about Smarties in this chapter.

7

OK, I know I lost the plot a little bit there with the Smarties. And look, that's probably the most accurate use of the expression "losing the plot" ever. Even I don't know what I was supposed to be on about any more.

Oh yes, global pandemic.

Reasons for why I started counting to a million.

Right.

I'll see if I can go a bit quicker.

• • ★ • •

By the end of the weekend I had found out quite a lot about the coronavirus. I kept thinking of questions to ask my parents, but I didn't want them to think that I was worried about it. Apparently this is the most important thing about the whole pandemic: don't let the children worry.

So I got my holiday journal out of the drawer. Last summer Mum made me write a sentence a day. She was afraid I would forget how to read and write during the holidays, and that I'd arrive in Year 4 like some sort of caveman.

There were lots of spare pages in the journal, so I started writing down my questions:

- How is a virus not really alive?
- On a scale of one to ten, how not worried am I supposed to be?
- If you lose your sense of taste, could you eat raw onions and not cry?
- If we can't get any toilet paper, what will we use instead?

By writing down my questions, I could ask a

few at a time when the subject of the coronavirus came up. That was better than asking them when I thought of them, which was pretty much all the time. It was important that my parents knew I wasn't worrying.

I also started watching the news a bit more. When Dad finished his dinner, he would often put the news on. Sometimes I would watch with him, which annoyed my mum.

"Why are you filling his head with this right before bedtime?" she would say, as the screen showed terrible scenes of a hurricane or a fire, or a politician walking down a street with a folder.

"It's important for Max to understand that the world isn't all beer and skittles," Dad replied.

That's an expression that makes no sense. I know perfectly well that the world is not all beer and skittles. Also, beer is disgusting, so it's not a very good description of a happy world. I asked Dad what he meant and he said it was the bowling skittles, not the sweets. It still doesn't make any sense.

The point is, Dad thought it was healthy for me to know a little bit about what was going on in the world. He wanted me to know who the politicians were, and who it was that was running the country into things. There was a limit though, and sometimes he saw the "Coming up tonight" bit at the start and turned it off.

My favourite thing about the news was Bea Hixby. She was a community reporter, so she always did stories that were about ordinary people. I liked her because she had an X in her name and so straightaway she was on my team. She also had a nice face.

Sometimes I'd be reading or playing with my Lego and not really paying attention to the news. Then I'd hear the newsreader go, "Our community reporter, Bea Hixby, has the details," and I'd stop what I was doing and watch. You say her name Bay-a, by the way. Not Bee-a.

If I could choose anyone off the TV to be my friend, or maybe my big sister or something, I would choose Bea Hixby. There are lots of people on TV who are much more famous than reporters, of course, like footballers or rock stars, but that's not who I would choose.

Perhaps I have said too much about Bea Hixby. She's not my girlfriend or anything. She just has a nice face. And an X in her name.

That night, Bea Hixby was doing her reporting from a care home. She was explaining how the coronavirus was much more dangerous for older people. Lots of older people were being asked to stay at home and not see anybody, to make sure that they were safe.

I thought of something and felt a little rush of worry in my chest. We were supposed to be going to see Grandma and Grandpa during the holidays. This wasn't a question for the journal. It was a question for now.

"Dad, we will still be able to go and see

48

Grandma and Grandpa, won't we?"

"Oh," said Dad. It sounded like he'd just thought of it too. "No, I don't suppose we can now."

"Not even a quick visit?"

"I'm sorry, I hadn't thought as far as the holidays. I don't think we can see them."

Mum came into the living room carrying two cups of tea, and Dad turned to her.

"Your dad, with his heart; I presume he's going to be taking extra care?"

Mum nodded. "I guess so. We won't be able to visit them, Max. I'm sorry."

So that was my holiday plans down the toilet.

Then I thought of something else. Some*body* else. Somebody who lived by himself and who didn't have a heart problem. I called him Grandad. Dad called him Dad. Mum called him Grandad Phil, but it's all the same person. He was going to be Official Gamesmaster at my birthday barbecue. We'd been planning it for

a while. Grandad was planning the games we would play with all my other friends. I'd been planning the special Official Gamesmaster hat I was going to make for him to wear.

"Grandad can still come to my party though, right? That's weeks away."

"Erm..." Mum and Dad looked at each other.

"I don't know, Max," said Dad hesitantly.

"Or even without Grandad, the party would still happen." That wasn't a question from me. That was a statement. There was a little wobble in my voice when I said it, coming from a much bigger wobbly feeling growing inside.

"I'm sorry, I just don't know."

"How can you not know?" I shouted, and I angrily jumped up from the sofa. "I thought you were supposed to be a doctor!"

I shouldn't have said that. I also should have chosen a better time to stand up, because that was the exact moment Mum was passing Dad his cup of tea. I knocked into her arm, and the hot tea sloshed on to Dad's knee and on to the coffee table. Mum and Dad both stared at me, shocked. Tea soaked into Dad's jeans, and the carpet, and the newspapers on the table. Drops had fallen on the TV remote.

Obviously, what I should have said then was "sorry", and then I should have helped to clean up. But it's too late for that now. What I shouted instead was, "You don't know anything, and you don't even care about my birthday!"

Well done me.

Dad didn't shout back. He just said, "I think you'd better go to your room and count to a hundred." And I did. Mum and Dad came to tuck me in and I said sorry, but I lay awake for quite a while, staring at the ceiling.

Oh, Bea Hixby, why did it have to be you bringing the bad news?

8

Monday came, and Mum dropped me off at school. When it was time to take the register, there were some names missing. Mahia wasn't there. Neither was Roman.

There was no point in avoiding the subject any more. Mrs Pine, the teacher, explained that some parents had taken their children out of school because of the coronavirus. The virus was more dangerous for some people, and not just if they were older. If you had a health problem, or if you were having a baby, it was super important that you didn't get the virus. Mahia had a brother who was often unwell, so her whole family were staying at home to keep him safe. The teacher told us that this was called "shielding".

I decided that "Shield Mode" was a better way of saying it than "shielding". If I heard a teacher say that someone was shielding, I immediately said "Shield Mode" in a cool robot voice, and soon everyone was saying it.

The next day we all had to use hand sanitiser on the way into school. There were three more children missing from the register, including James the Half-Friend and Ava who lives on my street. Everyone was talking about it in class and Mrs Pine had trouble making us all settle down. Then at assembly we heard that Mr Collins the PE teacher wasn't in either. Everyone else was just shielding, but he actually had the virus! He was the first person I knew who had got it, and suddenly the pandemic felt more serious. When we came back from assembly, the classroom was a lot quieter.

· ● ★ ● ·

At lunchtime, everyone was talking about Mr Collins and who else they knew who had the virus. Felix said his uncle had got Covid while he was in Italy on a business trip. Then Xavier said that his uncle and his aunt had both got it on a trip too. We weren't sure about that. Xavier is always repeating whatever other children say, but trying to make it sound more impressive.

Once I said that I had been to the cinema. He said straightaway that he'd been to the cinema the day before, and was going again that day. Another time Felix said his brother was getting a PlayStation 5, and Xavier said he had a PlayStation 6, even though that didn't exist yet.

Xavier still has to be in Team X because he has an X in his name and that's the rules. But I sort of wish he wasn't. Anyway, you say his name *Zavier*, so it's not even a real X sound.

I'm pretty sure he's a double-agent from Team Z.

I've tried to spy on Team Z a few times to try and find out. Unfortunately, Team Z are very cunning. Hazel and Zara never play with each other and don't even like each other. And Ezekiel and Zane are in different classes and they don't meet up either. This basically proves that they're up to something. Never being seen together is a perfect way to pretend that there is no Team Z, so they can carry out their evil plans without anyone suspecting.

Felix, Alex and I have some good ideas for spying on them, but it is quite difficult with Xavier around.

By the way, only X and Z have teams. That's because they're the best two letters. The leader of Team X is me because I invented it. Also, I'm the only one who gets messages from the mysterious Double X, who is the ultimate boss.

Amara desperately wanted to be in my team. We told her it wasn't possible, so she said, "Fine, I'll start my own Team A."

Felix said that Max and Alex would be on her team as well as on Team X, and that's obviously not allowed.

"Fine, Team M then!"

"But Max would still be in that too."

"Team R?" said Amara, and then we all started making pirate noises. "Arrr, Team Aaarrr!" And "Am*arrra*". That's why Amara's gang is called The Pirates.

We're allies with them. If there's ever a war or a showdown, Team X and The Pirates will join forces and be undefeatable.

It was Amara who got us all in trouble that day.

It was her idea to play coronavirus tag. The person who was "it" had the virus, and every time they tagged someone else they got the virus too. You were safe if you touched the bench and shouted "Shield Mode". The game kept going until there was just one person left, and then they were the Pandemic Survivor and the game started again.

We all liked the game and soon loads of us were joining in. We played it two times, and the second time I was nearly the survivor. There were only three or four children left, and about fifteen infected people chasing them. I had run to the far end of the playground to get away, and I was just making a crazy dash back to the bench when I saw Mrs Malik. She was striding towards us again, waving her hands in the air.

"Are you playing 'coronavirus'?" she said in her special telling-off voice.

"It was Amara's idea," replied about three children at once.

"I don't care whose idea it was," huffed Mrs Malik. "It's very insensitive!"

Nobody said anything.

"Don't you know there are children in this playground who are very worried about the virus, and you're turning it into a game? And poor Mr Collins at home sick. Is that a game to

you, is it?"

I looked at my shoes. They were black and there is not much else to say about them.

"Stop this game at once," Mrs Malik ordered. And then as she walked away, she added, "I hope you're all very ashamed of yourselves!"

As soon as she was gone we played it again. Exactly the same rules, except this time the game was called Zombies.

Standing in Shield Mode for a moment, I looked around the playground at the children who weren't joining in. Who was it who had told on us? Someone had gone to Mrs Malik to try and spoil the game. Classic Team Z behaviour.

9

All week my parents had been discussing whether they should take me out of school or not. In the end their arguments didn't matter, because on Wednesday the government announced that all the schools would close.

The floppy-haired Prime Minister made a speech on television, and we all watched it together. He was very serious, and told the whole country that the virus was extremely dangerous. He said everyone had to do something called social distancing, which is when you stand further apart from each other. His hands made tight fists and he banged the desk to show that he wasn't even joking.

Usually, the last day before the holidays is a happy day. Often we just watch a film and don't do any lessons. Friday wasn't like that. The teachers were very stressed. There was lots of rushing about, getting PE kits and work books to take home. Did everyone have a reading book? Had everyone written down their password for the online learning? Mr Abbot, the head teacher, gave a special assembly and told us that we were all part of one school family. Even though we couldn't be together, he wanted us to know that he cared about us.

In his talk, the Head said more than once that he didn't know when he'd see us again. I thought we were finishing a week early, and were going to get three weeks' holiday instead of two. But all the teachers were talking about a longer time than that. The school really was closing down.

· · ★ · ·

I expect most children have daydreamed about their school closing down. Sometimes in the afternoon I stare out the window and think about different ways that the school might disappear. Here's a list of some of the things I've thought about, before Mrs Pine tells me to pay attention:

- A meteor strike hits the school during the night and destroys it. All that's left is a huge crater, so the children fill the crater with water and it becomes a lake with beaches and pedal-boats. That's my favourite one.
- Once I was watching the news with Dad and there was a bit about a school that had a dangerous poison in the walls. Some kind of powdery chemical. They had to close the school to dig the poison out and then fix it up. I imagined that it happened at my school, and there was so much of the weird stuff that they had to knock the whole school

down. In my daydream the head teacher did it himself with a bulldozer, but in real life it would probably be a builder.

- There's a book in the school library called *My Teacher The Alien*. After I read it, I imagined all the teachers were aliens, and one day they were all beamed up to their spaceships in the middle of school. The children agreed not to tell the parents, so they still got dropped off each day. Then everyone just ran around and did whatever they wanted.

- Squirrels live in the trees on the other side of the fence. One day, hundreds of them took over the school. When the teachers came to open up in the morning, the squirrels threw felt-tip pens at them (with the lids off) until they ran away. An army of squirrels built a fence out of twigs and desks and PE equipment so that nobody could get in any more, and that was the end of school.

All of these imaginary versions of school closing are more exciting than the real one. The one situation I hadn't thought of was a pandemic, and that was the one that came true. It would have been a lot better with the meteor or the squirrels.

. . ★ . .

Even though I think about school closing down forever, I do like school really. I like my friends. I like the teachers. I like getting lunch on a tray. And I like learning, so that's pretty much most of school. Well, I like most of the learning. History and geography and science are fun. There are stories in English and I like those. Maths I'm not so sure about.

The trouble with maths is that you can do all kinds of interesting things with numbers, but you never do. You could be working out how many jelly beans you could fit in a bath. Or who would win in a race between a monkey riding a dog, and a dog riding a monkey. But you don't

get to do that sort of thing.

Instead, you get problems like "John has 48 pencils. He gives 5/6 to his friend. How many pencils does John have left?"

I have further questions: why does John have 48 pencils? I'm guessing that they are colouring pencils, but are there even 48 different colours of colouring pencil? Or does John have some that are the same? You can see that the problem is more complicated than it looks.

The answer is eight, by the way. Which only brings more questions: which eight colours is John keeping? Obviously if it was me, I'd keep the most important and most favourite colours. But what would John's friend say if he got all the boring or weird colours that are left?

"How do you spell turquoise?" I asked Mrs Pine when we were doing the question about John's pencils.

"Can we stay on task please, Max," she replied. "Art is this afternoon."

She had not understood the problem.

· ○ ★ ○ ·

Anyway, there wasn't going to be any more maths for a while, with the school closed. No more of anything for a while.

That made me happy and sad at once. And a little bit confused. Since I'm being honest, it even made me a bit scared – just a tiny bit. But not worried, because that wasn't allowed.

We lined up in the playground, right before they let the parents in to get us. Usually we play a game while we're waiting, where we try and step on each other's shadows. We have to do it sneakily because if Mrs Malik sees us playing, she tries to make us stop. That day she saw me leap on Alex's shadow. Right on his shadow head, with both feet. *Stomp!* And she didn't say anything. She just smiled. And then when she said goodbye to me a minute later, she looked like she might be about to cry.

I had a strange feeling then. I remember the

same feeling when I was learning to ride my bike. Dad was running next to me, pushing me along. Suddenly I realised that he had let go, and I was riding on my own. He was behind me, and I was riding away by myself. I didn't know I could do it – but I was. Now, could I keep going? Or would I panic and crash?

This feeling was a bit like that. It's hard to explain. Like John and his pencils. That's hard to explain too, but probably not very important. This felt hard to explain and also important.

· · ★ · ·

School was not the last thing to close. The supermarket was odd again on Saturday, but mostly it was like a normal weekend. By the next week though, every day there was a long list of things that had stopped or been cancelled.

The football had stopped. The cinema closed. You couldn't go to the swimming pool any more. The council put locks on the gates into the playground. Then all the cafes and pubs were shut.

And the tiny zombies weren't done ruining everything yet.

The Prime Minister made another speech, and I learned another new word: lockdown.

10

When somebody goes to prison, they are "locked up". When you're not supposed to leave your house because of a pandemic, it's called a "lockdown". Neither of these things have anything to do with up or down.

Things that are to do with up and down are called vertical. Things that are side to side are horizontal, which is easy to remember because it's got the word *horizon* in it. You probably know that already, but I'm putting it in because I want my book to be educational. Pay attention, because it might come up in the quiz later.

Since there's nothing vertical about lockdown or locking people up, both should be called a "lock-in". That would make more sense.

I told Mum this at breakfast time. She said that "lock-in" is already taken and means something else. I asked what it was, and she said, "Ask your dad."

I did. Dad said it was basically when people lock themselves in the pub, turn off the lights and drink all the beer. Then he said, "But you didn't hear that from me, all right?" And he winked.

Sounds dodgy to me. Beer is disgusting, as I have already said. And now you want to drink it in the dark? For no reason? Only grown-ups would want to do this.

Actually, "lock-in" isn't a good enough name either. We weren't locked inside our houses. We didn't have to dig an escape tunnel to get out.

In the end, I decided to call it "Shutdown". Like when you have to shut down the computer –

no more games for you. That's what the country was like, with everything closed. I know it's got the "down" back in it, but it sounds good when I say it in the robot voice that I use to say "Shield Mode".

· · ★ · ·

These were the rules for shutdown. They were explained to us by the floppy-haired Prime Minister in another one of his speeches:

- Don't go out.
- You can only go out for an hour of exercise or to go food shopping. Or to help someone who needs help.
- That's basically it.

While the Prime Minister was talking, I looked at his desk. There were no papers on it. I thought about all the other adults with desks that I knew – Mum's desk in the bedroom. Dad's at work. Mrs Pine. The ladies in the school office. The head teacher. All of them had papers on their desks. Lots of things to do. Some of them were in neat piles, some of them scattered about, but always papers. The Prime Minister didn't have any papers.

I decided there were two possible reasons why there were no papers on his desk. One was that he secretly wasn't doing any work. The other reason was that the coronavirus was so important that everything else had to wait. I imagined him sweeping big piles of papers off his desk in one go, and telling his servants to clear up the mess.

"I don't want to hear about any of this other stuff!" he shouted as he did it, in my imagination. "I have to tell the people to stay at home!" And then he sat down next to his flag, fluffed up his hair and talked to everyone through the TV.

I wonder if it's fun being Prime Minister, or if it's difficult.

I think I'd prefer to be an astronaut.

Straightaway, life was very different. The virus had changed everything. The whole world was closed. There was just me and my family left, in our house and our little garden. Sometimes we saw the woman who lived next door, and talked to her over the fence. Her children were grown up and gone, but I still called her Toby's mum. I'm guessing she had an actual name too. But she wasn't out much. It really did feel like we were the only people left in the world sometimes.

And it was OK. I did some reading with Mum in the mornings, and some maths on the computer. Mum's appointments with her clients had all been cancelled but she had to phone them instead, so I played with my Lego while she did her calls.

I called Grandad on a video call and showed him the truck I had made that looked like a normal truck but had secret spy headquarters inside. He showed me the birdbox he had made. It looked like a normal birdbox and didn't have anything secret inside, and I told him he should do something about that.

I called Grandad quite often. It was very different being shutdown all on your own. I didn't want him to get lonely.

A lot of Dad's appointments were cancelled too, and he actually came home early for a few days. It seemed to be always sunny, and we played football in the garden and went for bike rides.

Shutdown bike rides were really good. There was hardly any traffic about because everybody was at home, so Dad let me ride my bike in the road for the first time. I learned how to signal with my arm when I was going to turn, and we even went round the roundabouts on the housing estate down the road. I would have gone round and round the roundabout for ages, but the Prime Minister said you were only supposed to

73

be out for an hour.

Since Dad was home a lot more, we got to all eat together for a change. Mum and Dad cooked, and I'd set the knives and forks on the table outside.

We were OK.

The coronavirus had taken a lot of things away, but what was left was enough.

For a little while, anyway. As it turns out, the pandemic had more to take. Worse days were coming.

That sounds bad, doesn't it?

Don't worry. We're getting to the counting soon, if you're wondering when that's going to happen. But to get there, we have to get through a sad bit. Hold on tight!

11

My dad works at the hospital, as I mentioned already. Because he's an ear, nose and throat doctor, he works in the clinic. People come in and see him, and then the clinic closes at the end of the day and he goes home.

Not all doctors work like that.

Think about it. What if you get up to go to the toilet in the middle of the night, and because you're sleepy and confused, you turn the wrong way and fall down the stairs in the dark. Then you're lying at the bottom with your leg all broken. So you call an ambulance and they say, "Sure, we'll have the doctor

look at it in the morning." And you have to lie there all night?

Nobody wants that. That wouldn't work at all.

There are always doctors and nurses available if you need them. Any time of the day or night. Those doctors work shifts, which means they take it in turns to work in the very early morning, in the daytime, the evening or at night. So sometimes they are out all night or come home really late. Dad says I'm lucky that he gets to come home at a normal time, and so we get to see each other every day. Sometimes he works at the weekend, but not every single one.

Coronavirus made things much more complicated. Lots of people who got the virus were OK at home, but some got so sick that they needed to go to hospital. If too many people got sick in one place, then the hospital would start to fill up. Then they would need extra doctors.

Dad had warned me that if it got too busy at the hospital, he might have to be one of those extra doctors and do some shifts. That might get tricky, because he'd be working in the night and then sleeping in the day. I'd need to be extra quiet.

· · ★ · ·

I'm not a loud person, honestly. There are just a few things that I like to do that are noisy, that's all.

When I go up the stairs, I run with my hands as well as my feet, which my mum says sounds like a herd of elephants. When I come down the stairs, I go one at a time until I'm nearly at the bottom, and then I jump the last three. Mum says one day I'm going to go straight through the floorboards. This is nonsense. There is a carpet. If the floorboards crack, the carpet will catch me like a hammock. Hopefully.

I have guitar lessons and I'm quite good at remembering to practise. But that's not noise. That's beautiful music. I like to whistle while I draw. My other grandpa taught me. That is also

beautiful music and should not count as being loud.

I do enjoy kicking the football against the back wall, and Mum says this makes a thump-thump noise. That's Mum and Dad's fault. If they didn't want me to kick the ball against the wall, they should have had another child and I'd have had a brother or sister to kick it to instead.

My radio-controlled police car is a bit noisy, that's true. Especially if I put the siren on. But that's not me being noisy, it's the car. And I have to put the siren on to warn the traffic to get out of the way.

OK, if the football is on, I do sometimes shout at the TV. So does Dad. "Ref! Ref! Offside!" Things like that. That's quite an important part of watching football. Watching football isn't nearly as fun as playing it. If there haven't been many goals, shouting is often the best bit.

But am I a noisy person? Clearly not.

The first time Dad worked a late shift, he sneaked in at five in the morning and went to bed in the spare room. I forgot when I got up in the morning. I went humming down the hallway to the bathroom and Mum came bustling out to shush me. I tiptoed downstairs and remembered not to jump at the end. I watched TV with the volume turned down low.

"How long is Dad going to sleep for?" I whispered to Mum at breakfast.

"Until lunchtime," she replied, and so I had to stay downstairs and be very quiet all morning.

To stop myself from stomping by accident, I decided to put some extra padding on my feet. I crept into my room super quietly and I put on all my pairs of socks. It was about twelve pairs. I put the smallest ones on first, and the thick winter ones on last.

That made my feet quite big, so then I got some of Mum's socks and put them on. Then my feet were so big I could wear Dad's socks too,

and so I put them all on. My feet were like big rugby balls of pure silence. I tested them with a little jump up and down in the bathroom, and there was no noise at all. Total stealth feet.

Unfortunately, the stealth feet were a bit clumsy. As I was coming down the stairs I tripped over and fell down the last few steps, knocking into the banister and thumping on to the bottom stair. I was fine, so you don't need to be worried about that. I got up quickly and tried to get the huge multi-socks off before Mum saw them, and then I heard Dad from upstairs. "What was that? Everything all right?"

It was only ten o'clock, so Dad had not got enough sleep. Everyone was grumpy for the rest of the day. Dad was yawning when he went back to work in the evening, and nobody wants a tired doctor.

Mum told me I'd been silly and inconsiderate. I told her I was only trying to help, but she just raised her eyebrows at me. Then she was even more grumpy when she found that I had got the socks mixed up when I put them back, and she had to sort out her and Dad's sock drawers.

That was not a good day. I realised that night shifts were hard for Dad, but they were going to be hard for everyone else too. We were all going to live differently and keep quiet during the day. Like night creatures. Like hedgehogs. And, like hedgehogs, people might get spiky.

· · ★ · ·

For the next couple of days I tried harder to be less noisy. I did lots of reading. When I coloured in, I chewed a pen lid to make sure I didn't whistle. I thought of some other ideas for being quiet, like shuffling along in my sleeping bag like a caterpillar instead of walking. I even did sitting-down wees so that it didn't make loud splashing noises in the toilet. I managed to not wake Dad up, but it was very boring.

But this wasn't the worse thing that I warned you about earlier.

81

That happened in the second week of shutdown. Dad told us that there were lots of people at the hospital now with Covid. He was helping to look after them, and that meant that he was at high risk. It would be easy for him to catch the virus, and then when he came home, he might give it to me and to Mum.

The hospital knew that this might happen with lots of its doctors and nurses, so they had booked all the rooms in a hotel nearby. The hotel was letting them all stay for free. All the doctors and nurses could stay there instead of going home, and they could protect their families.

"Wait, so you'll be staying there? And not coming home at all?" I asked.

"It's not something I want to do," Dad replied. "It's to keep you safe. Both of you."

And so Dad had to move into the hotel.

The next day Dad packed a small suitcase with some clothes to wear and pyjamas. He chose a stack of books to read because there wouldn't be much to do when he wasn't working. I helped by getting the tablet and its charging cable so that he could do video calls with me every day. Then Mum drove us to the hospital in the car to drop Dad off. It's hard to park by the hospital so we stopped in the road. Mum and Dad had a long hug. Dad gave me a long hug. A car behind us beeped its horn to hurry us up. Then I got back in and we had to drive on. Dad stood by the grass and waved, and I waved back until we had gone all the way round the corner. Then Mum and I drove home without saying anything.

That was a bad day.

There were good things and bad things about school closing. There were good things and bad things about the shutdown.

But there was nothing good about my dad having to move out.

12

It was just me and Mum in the house now. We couldn't go anywhere. None of my friends could come over. It was just me and her, day after day. And like I said before, we're a bit different.

For starters, I am what Mum calls a "morning person".

That means that when the sun comes up, I get up. I'm like a bird. The sunshine comes through the curtains and it makes me want to sing. And eat worms.

Only joking about the worms.

Mum is not a morning person. It takes her a while to get going. She likes to lie in bed for a bit, and then shuffle about in her dressing gown. She makes coffee and stares out the window with it while it steams.

"What time do you call this?" says Mum as she comes yawning out of her bedroom, hair all sticking up everywhere.

"Daytime," I say, because it is. Let's not waste it with lying about.

"Do you have to sing quite so loud?" she grumbles.

Usually Dad would be up and getting ready, because his work starts a bit earlier than Mum's. As soon as Dad was gone to the hotel, Mum was suddenly in charge in the morning. I tried to not wake her up for as long as possible. I tried to get my own breakfast and tiptoe about. I tried not to talk too much while Mum was still doing the coffee-and-staring-out-the-window part of her day.

I really was trying.

I could tell that Mum was trying too.

Once we were all dressed and ready to go,

Mum and I would go for a short walk. This was like pretending to go to school or the office, even though it was still the holidays. We'd walk down the road and past Ava's house. Ava was new that year at school and didn't join in with the kind of games that I played, so she wasn't really on the friend list. Still, every time we walked past, I would look at her house to see if I could see her through the window. I never did, but it would have been nice to wave to somebody from school.

Even a teacher.

The daily walk cut through the churchyard at the end of the street, and back again down the next street along. This wasn't even our proper exercise hour, so it was probably against the rules. Mum said it helped her to focus and start the day, so I didn't say anything. But I kept an eye out for police cars, just in case. If one had come along, we could have quickly hidden behind a wheelie bin.

Mum was working from home, so once we had done our little walk, she got out the laptop. Sometimes we would sit at the dining-room table and I would do puzzles or read while she was doing emails and stuff. When it was time to do her calls or write her reports, she went to her "office", which was really just a little desk in my parents' bedroom. I was supposed to leave her alone to work then.

I mostly did.

Being a nutritionist, Mum helped people to eat better food and be healthier. I knew that she worked with the council, and also had clients. I imagined her having meetings where she checked that people were eating their five a day. Sometimes she'd have to tell them off for eating chips every day, or for having two puddings. That kind of thing. But when I used my spy skills to listen to Mum working, it seemed to be mostly typing on the computer.

I tried to leave Mum alone to work.

I honestly did. But then the batteries would run out on my police car. Or I couldn't find my blue colouring pencil. Or my favourite cup was in a cupboard that I couldn't reach. Or I'd look out a window and see a squirrel chasing another squirrel and I'd need to tell someone about that. Or the postman would come and I thought I should deliver the letters to Mum straightaway in case they were urgent. Or I'd be reading and I'd finish a chapter.

"I finished a chapter!" I shouted.

There was no reply. I went upstairs and opened the bedroom door.

"I finished a chapter," I said again.

"Er…" said Mum, still typing. "Yeah, that's…" Then she didn't finish her sentence, but sort of slumped a bit. Like a bouncy castle when they let the air out. "I'm sorry Max, I'm just really busy."

· ○ ★ ○ ·

I wondered if I was being annoying.

I don't think I'm an annoying person. I certainly don't *want* to be annoying. There are enough people like that already, like Xavier or Miles at school. But then I thought about it a bit. Miles likes to be a pest. He does it on purpose. So I know I'm not like Miles. But I don't think Xavier knows he's annoying. He thinks he's perfectly normal. What if I'm like Xavier? What if my mum thinks I'm annoying, and only loves me because I'm in her family and that's the rules?

I decided to do some experiments. First I stood and looked at myself in the mirror for a long time to see if I got annoyed at myself. I didn't. I felt good about that, but I wasn't sure it was scientific proof. Then I decided to make a survey. I got out a fresh piece of paper and wrote some questions in extra-neat writing.

(Please circle answer)
1. Would you say that Max can be annoying?
   Never   Sometimes   Always

2. From 1 to 10, how annoying is Max?

   1 2 3 4 5 6 7 8 9 10
3. How would you describe Max?

   Fun   Annoying   Sneaky   Clever
   Something else

Usually in a survey you ask lots of people. Because of the shutdown, there was only Mum around. It would have to be a survey of one. I took my neat questions upstairs and opened Mum's door.

"Mum, can you do my survey?"

Mum sighed loudly and turned around in her spinny chair.

"Is it important? Can't you see I'm in the middle of something?"

I said it wasn't important, and I put my survey down with her papers for her to do later.

· ● ★ ● ·

The rest of the day was good. Mum finished work and played with me in the garden. We made dinner and she let me help, after I'd given my hands a good wash to make sure there were no tiny coronavirus zombies on them. Then we did a video call with Dad. Then for pudding we looked up recipes on the Internet for cake-in-a-mug that you make in the microwave. I could see that they had loads of sugar in, but Mum seemed to have forgotten that she was a nutritionist for a moment and I didn't remind her. I even got two chapters of storybook at bedtime.

Mum didn't give me back the survey, but I still found out the answers. Later, by accident.

13

After I'd gone to bed, I was lying awake thinking about microwave mug cakes. I was wondering if you could use anything bigger than a mug, and whether a bucket would fit into the microwave. Then I thought I heard Mum crying.

Mum once told me that any mum can hear their child crying from a mile away. It's like a mum superpower. Grown-ups might not know this, but kids can hear their parents cry from a mile away too.

Your mum crying is never OK, unless it's at a wedding. Or a wedding in a movie. Or pictures of a wedding.

I got out of bed quietly. I tiptoed down

the stairs. Mum was sitting on the step by the back door, where the evening sun was shining on the back of the house and making it all golden. She was talking to Dad on the phone.

"It's so hard," she was saying. "He just wants my attention all the time. Every five minutes it's something else."

I knew it was me she was talking about, because who else could it be?

"He needs you. He needs his friends. It's not fair on him. Do you know he made a survey for me today? It's here…" And then I heard Mum sobbing as she tried to read Dad the questions.

I was trying to help, but my survey had made Mum really upset.

I went back upstairs. I lay awake for quite a while longer, and this time I wasn't thinking about buckets of cake.

· · ★ · ·

The next day Dad phoned me. Well, he phoned Mum's phone because I didn't have one because

I was only eight. While I talked to Dad, I hopped on my stepping stones, which were some spare bricks I had found by the shed and put on the grass.

"I know it's hard with just you and Mum," he said.

"I'm trying to be less annoying," I replied.

"You're not annoying, Max," Dad said quickly. "Mum doesn't think you're annoying. She loves you to bits. You know that, right?"

I did know that.

"Mum just has lots of things to do and lots of things to think about, that's all it is. She doesn't mean to be cross. She's worried about you, and about her work, and about me. Normally when she's stressed she'd go for a run or something, but right now she can't do the things that make her happy. And I'm not there to help."

I promised that I would try harder.

Dad asked me if I was OK, and I thought about it for a moment. I wanted to tell him that

I missed him, and that I was lonely, and that I really was trying. But I didn't want him to worry, so I just said, "I'm OK."

· ○ ★ ○ ·

At lunchtime Mum told me that she had been talking to her boss, and that they were going to try and pause some of her work for a little while. She would try and finish some things off in the next few days, and then she'd have more time to spend with me.

"And that will be a good thing," she added.

Then I remembered what Dad had said about Mum going running. I suggested that she could run and I could ride my bike, and hopefully she'd be able to keep up. We did that in the afternoon for our exercise hour. I'd never seen Mum doing her proper running because she always went on her own, but I was surprised. Mum was fast. I was the one who couldn't keep up. We went right around the estate two times and I was the one who got tired first.

When Mum went back to her room to finish her work, I was careful not to interrupt. I decided to do a little project to keep myself busy.

I got out my best pens and lined them all up on the dining table. Then I got a cereal box from the recycling bin and cut off the top and the bottom. I opened it into a big piece of cardboard and started to draw a big rainbow on it. Lots of children had made rainbows and put them in their front windows. It was to say thank you to the NHS – that's the National Health Service in case you don't know. My dad works for the NHS because he's a doctor, so I made my rainbow extra carefully.

My best pens have excellent rainbow colours and I coloured the rainbow stripes in the right order and very neatly. Because it was a serious picture, I didn't add any silly things like a smiley face sun. This was for the NHS and that's the opposite of silly. But then I forgot and added a drawing of Dad sliding down the rainbow on a surfboard, which is perhaps a bit silly.

I drew an arrow pointing to Dad and wrote Dr Ben Cromwell, which is Dad's doctor name.

Then I wrote, "You're my hero".

And then I burst into tears.

I wasn't expecting to cry, because colouring makes me happy, especially if it's with my best pens. I didn't expect to cry because I was eight and that's not something I do much unless I fall over. Somehow there was all this crying inside me and I didn't know it was there.

I'm a bit embarrassed telling you about it, but I said I would tell the truth.

The crying came up like a sneak attack, and some tears dropped on my rainbow. That made me cry even more, because I had worked so hard to get it perfect and now it was smudged. And I wanted to run up to Mum, but I didn't want to be annoying and interrupt, which made me cry even *more*. And anyway, I don't think I could even have explained why I was crying.

97

I ran down the garden instead, and didn't come back in until all the crying that needed to happen had happened.

When Mum came down from her work later I was working on a second rainbow. The first one was in the recycling because it got smudged. This second one was not as good.

"That looks lovely, Max," said Mum.

"No it doesn't."

"It does, it's very colourful."

"Of course it's colourful, it's a rainbow. It's not exactly going to be black and white, is it?"

"All right, sunshine," said Mum, opening some kitchen cupboards and getting ready to make tea.

"Don't call me sunshine!" I snapped.

Mum stopped and looked at me.

"What's got into you all of a sudden?" she asked. I felt really cross, because it wasn't all of a sudden. And my second picture wasn't as good, and she was acting like everything was fine even though it obviously wasn't. Dad wasn't here and I wasn't going to have a birthday and I'd even got the blue and indigo stripes of the rainbow the wrong way round because I hadn't been concentrating.

"Nothing!" I shouted. "You're so annoying sometimes!" And I slammed my pen down.

"Well, if you're going to be like that, I think you'd better go to your room and count to a hundred."

"Fine," I shouted as I stormed off up the stairs. "I'll count to a million!"

14

One. Two. Three. Four. Five. Six. Seven. Eight. Nine. Ten. Eleven. Twelve. Thirteen. Fourteen. Fifteen. Sixteen. Seventeen.

I'm not going to go on like that all the way to a million, don't worry.

But as you can see, the count had begun.

Later, people said all kinds of nice things about me when they talked about me counting to a million. They said that I was amazing, and a hero, and an inspiration. They said I should be very proud. But like I said at the beginning, there are parts of the story that I'm not proud of. The start of the count is one of those bits.

· · ★ · ·

You may have guessed by now, but my parents sometimes send me to my room to count to a hundred. "Count to a hundred and then come back and say sorry," they say. It's supposed to help me calm down. Usually, it works. The counting distracts me and by the time I get to a hundred I feel OK again. Sometimes if I've really lost my temper, counting to a hundred doesn't work at all and I just sit there fuming.

It's not always a hundred. Sometimes the adults say, "Take a breath and count to ten." And one time I got really angry and said a swear word to Dad, and Mum told me to go and count to a thousand. I didn't, because I couldn't be bothered and they forgot.

Counting to a million, that was my idea. If Mum thought she could send me away to count, I'd show her just how far I could count to. Further than she expected. Further than she wanted. Far enough to make her feel bad.

So when Mum came upstairs a little while later and stuck her head round the door, I said, "Four hundred and forty-eight, four hundred and forty-nine."

She told me it was time for dinner, and I came down from my bedroom. I counted each of the stairs. There are fifteen. I didn't count them from one to fifteen, I just rolled the count into my big count.

Mum had made beans on toast. I knew she was trying to be nice to me because, as a nutritionist, she is mostly against baked beans. Too much sugar and salt. I smiled and nodded instead of saying thank you, and said, "Five hundred and twenty-one."

Then I started counting my beans. I ate them one at a time, counting them as I poked them with my fork. Mum talked to me a bit and asked me questions, but I always replied with whatever number I was counting.

"Do you want to talk to Dad later?"

"Six hundred and twelve."

I wasn't trying to be difficult. I just didn't want to lose count and have to start again.

And OK, I was trying to be difficult.

In case you're wondering about the beans, there were a hundred and twenty-nine.

I don't know why you'd be wondering about the beans. It's not important.

Dad called later. I think Mum was expecting me to stop counting and talk to him. That's the kind of thing parents do. "He's being difficult," one of them would say. "You try talking to him."

Even though I sort of wanted to talk to Dad, I also knew that it was Mum's plan. She would have sent a sneaky "He's being difficult" text message and asked Dad to call. But I was not a problem that needed to be fixed. I was a boy

who was a bit angry, and a bit upset, and who was counting to a million. And Dad was in the middle of a shift, so he didn't have time for a big chat anyway. He turned on the video call and I could see that he was in the staffroom at the hospital. I had been in there when I visited him at work once.

"How was your day, Max?" he asked.

"Nine hundred and fifty-two."

"Ah yes, Mum said you were counting to a million."

See? The sneaky text. I knew it.

"Nine hundred and fifty-five," I said.

"Well, it's nice to see your face anyway, Max. You don't have to reply if you don't want to. I'll do the talking for both of us." And then Dad chatted away as if it didn't matter at all that I was only replying with numbers.

After a couple of minutes I heard some people come into the room behind Dad, and Dad turned to them.

"Hey, Doctor Grace," he said. "Come and say hello to Max."

A friendly-looking woman appeared on the screen next to Dad.

"Hello, Max," she said. "Your father has told me so much about you."

"Nine hundred and ninety-one."

The woman laughed.

"Max is counting to a million," said Dad, while I kept quietly counting.

"Oh really?" laughed Dr Grace. "And where are you up to?"

"Nine hundred and ninety-four."

"Keep going. I want to hear you reach one thousand."

I counted the rest out loud, and when I said "one thousand" Dad and Dr Grace both cheered.

"I'm privileged to hear you count your first thousand," said Dr Grace. "Only nine hundred and ninety-nine thousand more to go."

When she said that, I stopped counting for a moment. Nine hundred and ninety-nine thousand to go?

15

Confession time: when I started counting to a million, I didn't actually know how big a million was.

I thought that every number that was big enough to have a name just had an extra zero at the end. A hundred had two zeros and a thousand had three zeros. Obviously the next one up was a million and would have four zeros. And so on, like this:

A hundred: 100
A thousand: 1,000
A million: 10,000
A billion: 100,000
A trillion: 1,000,000

That would be sensible and logical. But no! Apparently that's not how it works. Instead, it goes like this:

A hundred: 100

A thousand: 1,000

A million: 1,000,000

A billion: 1,000,000,000

A trillion: 1,000,000,000,000

I'm telling you, the people in charge of the English language need a good kick in the pants.

Billions and trillions have so many zeros on the end that it's getting ridiculous. What could you ever do with a billion of anything? Nobody even needs numbers that are that big!

Basically, what I thought was a million was actually ten thousand. A real million is a hundred times bigger than that. A real million is one thousand thousands. Count to a thousand, and then do it one thousand times, and you've got a million.

That is a lot bigger than I expected.

On the first evening, I kept counting as I loaded the dishwasher. Mum went into the living room and turned on the news. It had already started and they were talking about a hospital and how busy it was. Mum pressed the mute button on the remote control, the button that takes away all the sound. I peeked through the door, and I could just see Mum sitting on the sofa. She was staring at the screen, watching with the sound off. Her fingers were twisting the ends of her hair, which is something she does when she's worried. She didn't notice me and I went back to the dishwasher and clinked the plates a bit even though I was done.

How bad was it at the hospital? Was it Dad's hospital? I turned on the dishwasher and heard the little whoosh from the water jets coming on in the dark inside the machine. I felt a whoosh inside me at the same time, like a whoosh of worry. I started counting again.

I counted right through bedtime. The only time I stopped was when Mum turned the news sound back on and I realised it was Bea Hixby. As she was a senior member of Team X, it was important to pay attention in case there was a secret message hidden in the news report.

And also she has a nice face.

But mainly I watched in case of the secret message, possibly from Double X. There wasn't one today, but you never know. I held the number I was on in my head, and started counting again as soon as Bea Hixby said, "I'm Bea Hixby, now back to the studio."

When bedtime came, I counted my way up the stairs and into my pyjamas and while I brushed my teeth. Mum said she wouldn't read to me unless I stopped counting, so I quickly wrote down 1,622 on a piece of paper. When she'd finished reading, she said, "Are you ready to turn off your light now, or are you going to read for a bit?"

"One thousand, six hundred and twenty-three," I said.

"OK then, goodnight."

"One thousand, six hundred and twenty-four," I replied, and I said the "twenty-four" bit in a singing way that made it sound a little bit like goodnight.

When Mum had gone, I got out my children's dictionary and looked up "million". It said:

Million: noun. A number indicating a thousand times a thousand, or 1,000,000.

Dr Grace was right. A million was massive.

Now I had a decision to make. Was I going to count all the way to a real million, or to my version of it that was actually only ten thousand? Or should I just stop?

On the one hand, I had told people that I was counting to a million. They would be suspicious if I stopped at ten thousand. They might think that I didn't know what a million was.

On the other hand, a real million was a

very big number. Perhaps an impossibly big number.

Maybe the best thing was to forget it and get on with my life.

Ah yes, my life.

But what was that, exactly?

I was supposed to go and stay with Grandma and Grandpa, but that hadn't happened. I thought I would be going back to school at the end of the holidays, but it was staying closed. There was no football or swimming or music lessons. Normally if there was no school, we would have days out, at least go to the shops or to the library. Or I'd go and visit Grandad and take him to the playground. None of that was happening. Even my birthday party was cancelled. The shutdown just kept going even when it stopped being fun and interesting.

And now it was just me and Mum. Mum working, and worrying. Me trying not to worry. Trying not to be annoying.

I might as well be counting to a million.

· · ★ · ·

So when I got up the next day, I looked at my piece of paper. I crossed the room and opened the curtains, and said, "One thousand, seven hundred and one."

I counted while I got dressed, and counted down the stairs. As I was getting myself a glass of water, I noticed that the kitchen had little tiles around the sink. I counted all of them. Then I opened the back door and counted all the planks in the garden fence – down one side, and then back up the other to the house. This took me well into my second thousand, and by the time Mum came down for breakfast I was nearly at my third.

"Morning, Max," she said as she put the kettle on.

"Two thousand, eight hundred and ninety-two," I said.

"Oh, we're still doing that, are we?"

"Two thousand, eight hundred and ninety-three."

Then Mum said something that surprised me. It was, "Two thousand, eight hundred and ninety-four."

She kept counting with me, out loud, all the way until we got to three thousand. Then she gave me a high-five and a kiss on the head. And then she said, "Three thousand. That's pretty good, isn't it? Maybe enough for now?"

But I said, "Three thousand and one."

And Mum stared out the window for a bit while her coffee steamed.

16

I know some of you had been waiting for me to get to the bit where I start counting. Now that we're into it, I hope you're not disappointed. At this point I've got 997 thousands to go.

If you are disappointed, it serves you right for reading a book about a boy counting to a million. I mean, I put it in the title and everything. Perhaps you could read a book about boy wizards instead. It will be longer and harder though, just warning you. And it won't have a pandemic in it, or anyone doing an epic feat of counting.

It will have magic in it, which is good.

My count went very well on that first day. I counted all my own freckles up one arm and down the other. There aren't that many, so I did it four or five times. I counted in the garden as I hopped from one stepping stone to another. There's a shrub in the garden that is Mum's favourite and I counted all its leaves.

I counted all the bricks in the patio outside the kitchen door. Dad and his friend did the patio themselves when I was about four. They had to do some of it twice because they got the pattern wrong halfway through. It was a lovely sunny day and Grandad came to help and I learned my first swear word and then we had a barbecue. The patio is where I kick my football and I counted the kicks against the back wall. All of this counting was rolled into the master count. Having something to count helped me not to lose track.

I still did lose count a couple of times, when

I was distracted. Luckily, I wrote down where I was up to quite often and I didn't have to go back too far. That would be rubbish – imagine getting to 999,923 and forgetting where you were and having to start again! That definitely wasn't going to happen to me, and my count powered on for one, two, three days in a row. And when I was counting, I didn't think about coronavirus and I didn't miss Dad or worry about him getting sick.

The main distraction was Mum, because now it was her interrupting me. I'd be in the living room, counting all the tiny diamonds in the pattern in the wallpaper, and she'd come bursting in to ask if I wanted a snack. Then when I was counting my raisins and sunflower seeds (nutritionists are convinced that sunflower seeds are a good snack) she'd ask what I wanted to do for our exercise hour. Then we'd go for a walk and I'd be concentrating on counting my steps, and Mum would ask if we wanted to go

home or go round again.

Honestly, she just wanted my attention all the time. Every five minutes it was something else.

I think it was because her work had given her less to do, like we discussed. That was so she could spend more time with me, but now I was busy. I had a project and I was the one who should not be disturbed.

I think it was also because I was only speaking to her in numbers. All day, every day, all I said was numbers.

Even when Dad phoned, I just counted. I could see that Dad wanted me to talk to him, but if I started talking I would stop counting. And when I stopped counting I felt that little whoosh inside me, like all the jets of worry starting up inside my heart.

After four days Mum stopped talking to me, and I just counted to myself for almost the whole day. She even put my food on the table and then ate hers in the living room and watched the news. She didn't say anything to explain, she just turned on the TV and it was as if I wasn't even there.

That made me stop counting my pasta shells. I wrote down the number I had got to and just focused quietly on eating for a moment. Two things came into my mind then that I should have thought of earlier. Maybe if I was older I would have thought of them, but I was still only eight then. And even though I have some very useful skills, I can't read grown-ups' minds.

The first thing I realised was that Mum wasn't happy about my counting. It might actually be making her sad, and I didn't want to make her sad. Then I remembered that when I had started counting, that was sort of what I wanted to do. I'd wanted to make Mum feel bad by counting much higher than she told me to.

My original, angry plan was working. I was making Mum feel bad. Except that I didn't want

119

to do that any more. I still wanted to count to a million, but I wanted Mum to be proud of me for doing it.

The second thing I remembered was that it was nearly the weekend, and that meant the end of the holidays. On Monday school was supposed to restart. Because Dad was a doctor I could go back to actual school if I wanted to, but none of my friends would be there. I was going to start home-school with Mum instead. That meant that the count would have to end on Monday, and I was only on 57,802. I was not going to make it to a million by Monday, and then what? Fit in the counting after school? It would take me the rest of my life!

I decided that Operation Million, because that's what I was calling it now, would need my parents too.

Feel free to pause and say OPERATION MILLION a few times in different voices until you find the best way to say it. I did when I thought of it. My final choice is quite similar to the voice I use to say "Shutdown" and "Shield Mode" but not quite as roboty.

Got one? Now you can use it in your head whenever you read OPERATION MILLION. Or even out loud if you're reading this out loud. I'll write it in capitals to remind you to read it properly.

· ∘ ★ ∘ ·

When I'd finished my pasta, I looked over to Mum to check if she'd finished as well. Her plate was on the coffee table. I went quietly into the living room and climbed up on to the sofa next to her, and nuzzled into her shoulder.

"Oh, hello you," said Mum.

"Hello Mum."

"You're speaking words again, bless you," she said, and she gave me a big squeeze.

I decided to wait another day before I told Mum that we needed to cancel home-school.

17

As you know already, I like school. The first day back after the holidays is always quite exciting. You get to see your friends again and hear what they've been up to. Somebody might have a new game, or come into school with a cast on their arm. Or maybe someone has seen a film we're not old enough to see yet and you get to hear about it. Sometimes there's a whole new person arriving in class, and you have to be nice to them because they haven't got any friends yet.

The start of this new term wasn't like that.

School was supposed to restart, but

not actually at school. Instead, they had put the lessons and worksheets on the school website. You had to do it yourself, with no teacher and no friends. Just the learning, all by itself.

I was pretty sure that counting to a million would be better than that. More educational, even. So all the next day I waited for a good time to talk about school.

· · ★ · ·

It was a good day of counting. And now that I was saying words to Mum, things definitely felt better. Dad was clearly relieved to hear words from me as well. We told each other about what we'd been doing that day. Dad said he was all right, but tired. Long days and not enough sleep.

I asked him if there was anything we could do to help and he said that some people were dropping off snacks and drinks for the NHS workers. We could join in with that. He also said that people on the news talked a lot about the doctors and nurses, and forgot to mention the cleaners, the porters, the healthcare assistants, all the people who worked in the kitchens and the laundry at the hospital, and lots of others. Everybody was working extra hard. "If you bring in some snacks, bring them in for all of us," Dad said.

When it was time to finish, Dad added one more thing. "Before I go, let's count the next hundred together." So we did, picking up from 70,800 and counting to 70,900.

· · ★ · ·

Up at the top of our house there is a loft. It's mostly got empty suitcases in it, and insulation that looks fluffy and fun to roll on, but is actually very itchy. I learned that it was itchy by rolling on it because it looks fluffy and fun.

It was Dad's fault for not telling me, that's what Mum said. Several times. It was one of those days where she said, "What were you thinking, Ben?" and Dad was in the doghouse.

Except he was in the loft. Not in the doghouse. It's an expression.

Anyway, there's also a window in the roof. Dad put a big old box under it and you can sit on it and look out of the window. From high up in the roof you can see across all the neighbours' gardens and down the road to the churchyard. At night it's a good place to look at the stars.

Or *count* the stars, if you're after things to count.

Once it got towards bedtime, I asked Mum if she could open the loft as a special treat. "There won't be any stars out until well after your bedtime," Mum pointed out, but she still opened the hatch and put up the ladder for me. We climbed up and both sat on the box, leaning on the edge of the window. There was a totally clear blue sky above us. No stars to count, no clouds either.

"Dad and I sat here when we first moved into this house," she said. "Before you were born. It

was later in the summer and we did look at the stars then. We sat here and had a glass of wine."

"That's nice," I said.

"Yes, it was very romantic."

I knew where stories like this go. If there's wine and stars involved, it usually ends up with grown-ups kissing and there was no need for that.

"You know, the word romantic is made up of 'Roman' and 'tick'," I said. "Like a 'tick', or a flea, but from Roman times. Why is that?"

"That's…" said Mum. "That's a very good way to ruin the word 'romantic'." Then she laughed, and I thought now might be a good time to ask a difficult question, while she was full of happy memories and laughing.

"Mum, you know home-school is supposed to start on Monday?"

"Yes, and don't you worry. I've got the time off work to help, and we're going to do great."

"Well, what if we didn't have to do proper

lessons? What if I did an extraordinary but educational project instead?"

"Hmm," said Mum. She said it in a way that wasn't a definite no. I couldn't decide if that was a good sign, or whether she was working out how to say no nicely. "I don't know about that," she said eventually. "I suppose it would depend on the project. Did you have something in mind?"

"I was thinking of something like counting to a million."

"Is that educational?" asked Mum.

"Of course. Think how amazing I would be at maths by the end of that."

Mum wasn't convinced. "You'd be good at counting," she said. "That's not the same thing as being good at maths."

We looked at the sky in silence. There wasn't much to see in it unless you like the colour blue, and luckily I do.

"Why do you want to count to a million so

badly?" Mum asked, which was a fair question.

"Because it's epic," I replied.

"It is," she agreed.

I wondered what else to say. Just because something is epic doesn't mean you can skip school to do it. My Minecraft castle is epic and I don't get to stay at home and build that all day. I wondered if I should tell her about the whoosh, but we all know how important it was for children not to worry. That was my parents' biggest thing. They had enough to worry about without worrying about me worrying.

"The counting helps me," I said quietly.

"What does the counting help you with, Max?" Mum put her arm around me.

"I miss Dad."

"Me too."

Mum didn't say anything else, and we sat there for quite a long time. Long enough for Official Bedtime to pass by unnoticed, and I didn't point this out. Mum can sit for ages without saying anything. Usually it's me that has to say something before I explode. But this time it was her who spoke first. She suddenly sat up straight and pointed at the sky.

"Oh look, there's a swift!"

There was indeed a bird flashing high above the garden, doing giant scribbly loops in the sky.

"I'm sure that's the first one of the year," she said, and then she pointed out three or four more. They were all joining in with the looping.

We watched them together as they swooped and dived. Their wings hardly moved, like they weren't even trying to fly. They just steered about the sky like they owned the place. It looked like fun. I wondered if they were child swifts, mucking about before bedtime. Any minute now the adult swifts would tell them to come inside for bed.

I noticed that sometimes the swifts flew upwards with their wings tucked back, and it

made them into a kind of M shape. Sometimes they flew sideways and it made a kind of X shape.

I suddenly realised something amazing. It was a signal! The swifts were in Team X and they were here to help.

I didn't know how yet, but I somehow knew they were.

We sat and watched for a bit longer. Then Mum said, "Did you know swifts never touch the ground? It's true. They only land when they're nesting. Otherwise, they're up there the whole time."

"And they never get tired?"

"They sleep while they fly," said Mum.

That was a clever skill. I wish I could fly while I sleep. Or just fly. Just flying without being asleep would be fine.

"These ones have just flown all the way from Africa. Right across the Sahara Desert, across Spain and France. All without stopping. They'll have their babies and then in a few weeks they'll be gone again. We have to enjoy them while they're here."

"That's amazing, Mum," I said, and then I realised what the signal was that the Team X swifts were sending me. "You wouldn't expect something so little and so ordinary to attempt something so epic."

Mum nodded. And then a few seconds later she said, "You know what? Do it. You count to a million."

I punched the air a little bit and said, "Thanks, Mum." But in my mind I grew wings and shot up out of the window, soared into the sky and high-fived all the swifts.

18

I wondered if Mum knew how big a million is.

I mean, she probably didn't think that it was a one with four zeros, like I did. (And in fact, I still think a million should be that. Don't think I've forgotten, Dictionary People – you'll be hearing from me later.) But she might not have known just how big it was or how long it would take. But it's too late now. I had PERMISSION. I was going to count to a million.

Before I got too excited, the next day Mum reminded me that she had said yes without talking to Dad about it. He might still disagree, and we also needed to decide *how* I could count to a million. It might not be all in one go, which was of course what I wanted to do. We all talked about it at breakfast time with Dad on the video call. Dad thought it was a great idea and I should definitely do it, but I had to see it as a long-term project. It could fit in around my home-school – maybe lessons in the morning and counting in the afternoon.

This was not the plan.

"You've been counting for five days," said Dad. "And your total is?"

"Seventy-four thousand," I reported.

Dad started doing some maths on a bit of hotel paper. "So, seventy-four thousand in five days is fourteen thousand or so a day. If we divide a million by that we can see how long it's going to take you. And that would be…"

Some maths went on. I won't put it in. I don't want my book to be quite as educational as that.

"Right," said Dad eventually. "You want the answer?"

I nodded.

"At this speed it will take you sixty-two days. You'll still be counting in two months."

"OK," I said.

"And that's all you'd be doing. No time for TV or friends. That's two months of just counting, every day."

"OK."

"That's it? OK?"

"Yep."

"You might be back at school long before two months is up," pointed out Mum. "And then you'd have to count in your spare time anyway."

"All the more reason to get ahead while I can," I replied.

"I'm not sure your teachers will agree," said Dad, which was a reasonable thing to say.

"We don't need to tell them," I replied, which was also a reasonable thing to say.

And so Monday came, and I was still counting – for now. That's all Mum and Dad could agree to, at the end of the discussion. "For now" was good enough for me.

· ● ★ ● ·

Dad wasn't right about the sixty-two days though. I had realised something. It was going to be longer than that.

You see, counting to a million is a bit of a trap. The numbers get longer and harder to say as you go on.

Let me give you a little experiment to show you the problem.

First, count from one to ten as fast as you can. Done?

I bet it was fast, like onetwothreefourfivesix seveneightnineten almost in one long word.

I've timed myself counting to ten, and I can do it in under two seconds. Counting super fast like this is how some children cheat in hide and seek. It's the kind of thing Team Z would do.

On to experiment number two. Count from 77,770 to 77,780 as fast as you can.

Now you see the problem.

In both experiments you've counted ten numbers. But in the second one it takes waaaaay longer and it's much easier to make mistakes. There's a simple reason why.

When you say "one" or "two", it's just one short word each time. It's different when you have to say "Seventy-seven thousand, seven hundred and seventy-one. Seventy-seven thousand, seven hundred and seventy-two."

I noticed this problem once I got to seventy-seven thousand. I also noticed that of all the numbers, seven is the only one that has two syllables. All the rest are quicker to say. Seven is now my least favourite number. Thank goodness I was eight.

I was so relieved when I got to 78,000, and then a bit later to 80,000 and I could stop saying "seventy" so many times.

I hadn't told my mum and dad that I had found this trap in counting to a million. They weren't convinced about OPERATION MILLION in the first place. If I told them that it might be a lot longer than two months, they would definitely make me stop.

To be honest, I wasn't even sure if I wanted to keep going myself. Whenever I came around to the seven hundreds again – 81,700, then 82,700 – I remembered that I would eventually get to the real seven hundreds: 700,000. They would go on forever.

One day, deep in the future, I would have to say the most hated number of all: 777,777. All the sevens. Seven hundred and seventy-seven thousand, seven hundred and seventy-seven.

My nemesis.

This evil number began to spoil the fun of counting. Even writing it just now made me shudder.

Do you want to know something else? Something that confirms the evil power of the sevens?

Take a good long look at the number 7.

It's in disguise, but it is basically a Z.

19

All that week I kept counting. I found new ways to keep going. One was the Minecraft count, where I counted each block as I chopped tunnels with my diamond pickaxe. Or I counted all the little squares on Dad's chequered dressing gown, which I had started wearing in the morning even though it was way too big for me.

Food was often helpful too. Mum made rice and a curry, and I counted every single grain of rice on my plate while Mum grumbled about it going cold. I put my hula hoop on the ground and counted every blade of grass inside it. I was there for so long without moving that Mum came and put sun cream on the back of my legs so I didn't get sunburned.

To make things more interesting, I decided that every thousand with a nine in it would be musical, because I was nearly nine. So 109,000, and then 119,000, and then 129,000 and so on. I would sing the numbers, sometimes while playing my guitar. It was jazz, basically. Extraordinary music that would never be heard again by anyone.

Mum usually went upstairs while this was going on. Apparently she doesn't like jazz.

I passed my first 100,000 over the weekend. As I had worked out already, I now had to say "a hundred and" at the beginning of every number. I would have to say this a hundred thousand times. And then I would have to say "two hundred and..." a hundred thousand times until I got to 300,000.

This is the curse of counting to a million.

If I stopped to think about it, I started to wonder if a million was impossible. So I didn't stop. Not yet.

· · ★ · ·

One of the reasons that I didn't want to stop counting was that it was my birthday that week. When I was counting, I didn't think about coronavirus. I didn't think about Grandad all on his own. I didn't think about my dad. When it felt like everyone else in the world was hiding away from the virus, Dad had to put on his protective equipment and go in to where the sickness was. I was worried about that. Of course I was, and the counting helped me to forget.

It also helped me to forget about my glitched birthday.

You know what it's like at school. Everyone talks for months about their birthday parties, and who's going and what you're going to do. Last year I had a party with four friends and we went to the bowling alley and then to Nando's,

which is a chicken restaurant if you haven't been there. I had invited Felix, Alex, James the Half-Friend and Amara. (James is a half-friend because my mum and his mum are best friends and so he always gets invited, even though I never play with him at school.) While we were in Nando's Felix went to the toilet. He came back all excited because he had seen the Arsenal footballer Hector Bellerin at another table.

Then Mum said, "Are you sure? Because Hector Bellerin is a vegan and I don't think he'd go to Nando's." Felix was amazed. His mouth dropped open and I could see the half-chewed sweetcorn in it. He is an Arsenal fan and just had total respect for Mum because she knew who Hector Bellerin was.

Mum knew because she is a nutritionist. Part of her job is to help sports people with their diets, so she knows the names of any famous ones who are vegan or vegetarian.

When we'd finished our chips, all four of us

sneaked round to have a look. We peeked round from behind a pot plant. I don't really know what Hector Bellerin looks like, so I wasn't sure. He wasn't wearing an Arsenal shirt or the long socks that footballers always wear. Still, we told everyone at school that we had seen an Arsenal footballer at my party as if it was a sure thing.

When Xavier heard, he said that the whole Liverpool team came to his party and that Mo Salah took him for a ride in his Ferrari.

· · ★ · ·

This year I was supposed to be having a barbecue, so lots more people were invited. Even Xavier. Everyone was going to come round to my house, and we would have games and ice cream, and Grandad was going to be Official Gamesmaster. Of course I had told everybody all about it and how great it would be, and everyone had been looking forward to it. I expect most children would have agreed that it was going to be the best party.

So it's pretty much guaranteed that there would be loads of children waking up on my birthday and crying because my party wasn't happening, not just me.

Mum did plan a little surprise though. She got up early and made fruit salad for breakfast, and I counted in the garden while she did secret preparations. When it was almost lunchtime, we got in the car and drove to the park on the other side of town. We walked to the playground, which was closed and locked up. The swings hung on their chains, waiting for the pandemic to be over. Mum spread a picnic blanket on the ground next to the playground fence and we sat down. She started pulling plastic boxes out of the picnic bag, and then she looked up and past me, and she smiled.

"Aha," she said. "I think you'd better turn around."

I did, and there was somebody in the

playground. It was Dad!

I wanted to run over and hug him but of course that wasn't allowed. Mum and Dad knew that everyone would want to hug everyone else, and that's why they had planned a picnic with a fence down the middle to remind us to keep at a safe distance. But Dad sat on the bench in the playground and we sat on our blanket, and it was close enough.

Dad looked a bit jealous of our picnic though. While we were feasting, he had a sandwich out of a packet from a vending machine at the hospital. And we all know what packet sandwiches are like. No matter what the filling is, the first thing you can taste is the mysterious flavour called "packet sandwich". It's like they spray it on at the sandwich factory.

There were presents too of course, and Mum had brought them all to the park so Dad could see. Lego and board games, because those were good activities for a shutdown. Grandma

and Grandpa had given me a science kit again, because Grandma is a scientist and is sure that I should be one too.

Grandad's present was quite small. I was old enough to know that the best presents aren't always the biggest, so I wasn't disappointed. I unwrapped it and found a little silver device. It was round, with four zeroes on the front and a silver button on the top. There was a note to go with it.

When I was fifteen, I got my first ever job as a bus conductor, it said. That seemed a bit young to be getting a job, I thought. But it was the old days and it was different then. *I used this tally counter to keep track of how many passengers had got on the bus. It's over sixty years old and it works perfectly, because things were made properly then. (Not like today, when everything is cheap and rubbish.) You will need it more than I will if you're counting to a million. Happy birthday and happy counting, Max! Grandad.*

There was also a PS: *I hope you like it. It's taken me three whole days to find it in all the junk in the attic and the spare room.*

I pressed the button. It clicked beautifully, and the little counter moved from 0000 to 0001. This was a really excellent present. I wished Grandad had been there so I could say thank you.

· ○ ★ ○ ·

My birthday wasn't what I was expecting, but it was still good in the end. It was great to see Dad again. The only bad thing was that it felt terrible to have to say goodbye at the end. Dad walked back across the playground, which still had nobody in it. He jumped over the fence on the other side and jogged back towards the hospital. He turned around and waved, and then started walking backwards, still waving.

"Don't walk into a tree!" Mum shouted.

I laughed because there were no trees anywhere near Dad, and Mum was being silly. I also laughed because the laughing made me

a tiny bit less sad to be saying goodbye to Dad again.

· ◦ ★ ◦ ·

When we got home, Mum asked if I wanted to play one of my new board games, but I was really missing Dad. I thought that counting might help, so I did that. Mum didn't seem to mind. I counted for an hour on my stepping stones, using my new tally counter. I wanted to get to 150,000 by the end of my birthday and I only had a few thousand to go. But the numbers were getting longer.

Now that my birthday was over, maybe I could stop at 150,000. Maybe that should be the end.

But my birthday had one more surprise in store.

20

After dinner I was counting again while Mum did the dishwasher. You're not allowed to do the dishwasher on your birthday. That breaks every rule of birthdays.

I had been lying on the floor, carefully counting the tiny woolly loops in the carpet. As I went along, I poked each one with a cocktail stick left over from the sausages on sticks we'd had at lunchtime. I had two thousand more to go before I got to 150,000 and I could probably make it if Mum let me stay up a bit late. Or if the numbers weren't so long.

Mum came in and put the news on, so I kept counting the carpet loops. The politicians and the scientists said their usual stuff. A man in a suit talked about money. I wasn't paying much attention because I didn't want to lose count. But I always had half an ear out in case something important came on.

Sure enough, the newsreader started a story about visitor attractions. They were all closed of course. There were no tourists. No visitors to attract. "To tell us more, here's our community reporter Bea Hixby at one of London's small but iconic museums."

I quickly scribbled down my total before Bea Hixby's nice face made me forget where I was.

She wasn't on the news every day. I guessed this was because being a reporter was only a pretend job, like it is for Superman. Superman pretends to work at the *Daily Planet*, but is actually busy saving the world. Bea Hixby pretends to be a news reporter, but is really on important Team X business the rest of the time. The main difference is that Superman is made up.

Here was Bea Hixby, on my birthday. It must be deliberate.

I listened carefully for a secret message.

"It's been a tough time for smaller visitor attractions," she said. "I've come here to the Sherlock Holmes Museum at two-two-one B Baker Street to find out how they're coming up with new ways to engage their audiences during lockdown."

That was an interesting place to be, the Sherlock Holmes Museum. That was obviously a clue. Sherlock Holmes always had the answers. And it was at 221B Baker Street. B for Bea. B for Birthday.

Then I saw it. It was the way Bea Hixby had said the address. She didn't say "two hundred and twenty-one B Baker Street". She said "two-two-one".

That was it! It was so much shorter.

I looked at my running total.

148,561.

You could say that as "a hundred and forty-eight thousand, five hundred and sixty-one". Or you could say "one-four-eight-five-six-one".

Genius!

With this shortcut I would zoom through those tricky numbers.

This was a secret weapon powerful enough to crush even the mightiest and ugliest of the sevens. I knew I was right to pay attention to Bea Hixby on my birthday.

I held my hand up by my face so Mum wouldn't see, and blew Bea Hixby a sneaky kiss. Which was OK because through the television counts as social distancing. And I was just in time, as the report was ending. Another second and my flying kiss would have landed on the newsreader instead.

· · ★ · ·

I was hoping to stay up late as a birthday treat, and I didn't even have to ask. It was a Thursday and there was a new thing that happened every Thursday. You might have done it too if you were in the shutdown. At eight o'clock, everyone came out on to their doorstep and clapped for the NHS.

This was quite exciting, because Dad works for the NHS and so all the neighbours were clapping for him. And also because we got to see the neighbours. Really, we barely saw anyone during the shutdown. We hardly saw my friends, because I hadn't got any of their phone numbers to call them. Well, except James the Half-Friend, but that was our mums who were talking really. Nobody came over, and we couldn't go anywhere. So it was quite special to stand in the doorway and see actual people.

Because it was exciting, I was always the first one out into the street. This Thursday I stood out the front and counted the bricks on the

153

driveway with my new ticker. I was counting fast so I could get to my target before bedtime, and my new counting system was working well. "System 221B", I call it.

To be honest, I was probably ten minutes early for the clapping. But being early was lucky, because as I was counting driveway bricks, my neighbour Toby came by.

When I was little, Toby was the boy next door. I would see him over the fence with his friends, in their smart uniforms from big school. Some teenagers can't be bothered with younger children, but Toby was friendly to me. We would talk over the fence. He was always accidentally kicking his rugby ball over into our garden, and I would throw it back to him.

I suppose he had to be friendly to me. If he wasn't, I might not have given his ball back.

Toby didn't live next door anymore because he had gone off to university. But here he was, coming back from a run. He pulled his headphones out from his ears and said hello.

"What are you doing back?" I asked.

"Uni has closed," he said with a shrug. "Everything's going to be online now, so I thought I'd come home. What's new with you?"

"It's my birthday today," I said. "That's what's new. Also I am counting to a million."

"Wow," said Toby. "That's amazing. What number have you got to?"

"Nine."

"Nine? I take it back, that's not amazing at all."

"No, that's my birthday. I have got to nine, with the being alive."

"Oh, I see. Congratulations on that."

"OPERATION MILLION is currently on 149,650."

"OK, that is highly impressive," said Toby, sitting on the doorstep to wait for the clapping. "You must be very, very bored."

Just then his front door opened and his mum

stepped out. My mum came on to the driveway. The neighbours opposite appeared at the upstairs window. I hopped to the kerb and looked down the road to see who else I could see. A few doors down I could see Ava and her sister, and I waved to them.

As if by magic the clapping started.

21

At the beginning of my story I mentioned that not many people have counted to a million. In fact, there might only be one. I looked it up on the Internet and I found it on a website of world records. A man called Jeremy did it, and there is a video of him reaching a million. It happened in 2007, which is so long ago on the Internet that the video is almost in black and white. When he gets to a million, he does a strange chicken dance.

Counting to a million is easy, really. You just start, and you keep counting until you get there. Anybody could do it. Almost nobody does though, and there are a few reasons why:

- It's really quite boring.
- It takes a very long time.
- You almost certainly have more interesting things to do.

That's about it really. It's not a long list, but those are pretty good reasons not to do it.

If you're an adult, you might have a job to go to. Then your boss is definitely not going to give you time off for pointless counting. If you're a child, you have school. Even if you spent the whole summer holiday on it, you might not be able to get all the way to a million. Not all in one go.

In case you still hadn't understood this, a million is a really big number.

That is a problem for this book about counting to a million.

There are some interesting things at the

beginning. Some fun things happen at the end, which I won't spoil by telling you about them yet. In between, there's mostly just a lot of counting.

Days and days of counting.

Weeks and weeks.

It really is quite boring. It takes a very long time, and you almost certainly have more interesting things to read about. Like boy wizards, or space travel. Submarines. Robots. Dragons.

Or boy wizards in submarines fighting robot dragons in space.

· · ★ · ·

I have some definite goals for this book. When I think about what I want it to be, it should be:

- Fun – yes
- True – yes
- Educational – a bit
- Boring – no

It's the last one that I'm worried about now

that we've got properly into the counting. I will need to skip ahead to the best bits of what happened next.

· · ★ · ·

The good news is that System 221B worked very well. My counting speed had gone up and I didn't think it would take sixty-two days like Dad had guessed.

The less good news was that Mum had got in touch with the school to tell them about the count. I suppose it had to happen eventually. She said the teachers were going to talk about it and we needed to have a meeting with the school.

The meeting was a couple of days later. I prepared by writing a list of reasons why counting to a million was a good idea that should be allowed. Then I folded it neatly and put it in my pocket. I even put my school uniform on for the first time in weeks. I thought it might help the teachers to understand that counting to a million was a sensible idea from a sensible person.

Mum and I sat at the kitchen table with her laptop. We clicked to join the meeting, and I saw that it was Mrs Malik and Mrs Pine. I was hoping it would be just Mrs Pine, who was my actual teacher. Mrs Malik was head of year, and also head of fun-spoiling and game-stopping. She had probably been looking forward to this meeting so she could crush my joy.

But that wasn't what happened.

"Your mum has told us all about your project and why you're counting to a million," said Mrs Pine, when they had finished saying hello and noticing that I was wearing my uniform. Mum looked at me and smiled. I realised that she might have already done the convincing earlier.

"This is an unusual idea," said Mrs Malik. "But these are unusual times."

They said I could keep counting as long as I

didn't fall behind on my learning. If I could do one hour of lessons each day, that would be enough if I was focused.

Just so I didn't arrive back at school like some sort of caveman.

An hour of school was not ideal, but it was OK. I tried to get it done as early as possible so I could get on with counting. Grandad offered to help, since he wakes up early like I do. He would test me on my times tables. We would talk about nouns and verbs. Sometimes he would get distracted and tell me stories about when he was at school, but mostly he was on task and well behaved. Then Grandad got a cold and Mum took over the lesson hour. Which was fine, except that we had to start later, and I often had to wait patiently while Mum stared out the window with her coffee.

· ● ★ ● ·

There was another bit of good news. A few days after my birthday I was getting towards a quarter of the way into a million. Mum had sent me outside because I had got to the musical section of the day's count, probably 229,000. I wasn't on guitar this time. It was a sort of rap music that I was doing. Maybe Mum doesn't like rap.

I was rapping on the lawn, with Grandad's tally counter in my hand, when I heard someone behind me.

"Hey, Max!"

It was Toby, leaning on the fence like he used to do. I held up my finger to ask him to wait, and then scribbled down my running total.

"You know my trampoline?" said Toby.

I did. He used to sit on it with his friends after school. Teenagers don't bounce on trampolines, I've noticed. They just lie on them with their friends and talk.

"I went to jump on it the other day, and my feet touched the ground underneath. I guess I'm too heavy for it these days."

Toby was very big, that was true. I think rugby makes you that way.

"Yeah. I guess you can still lie on it though," I said, pretending I understood why teenagers would do that.

"True, but I was wondering if you wanted it," said Toby. "I reckon it would help with OPERATION MILLION, if you counted your bounces."

"I think it would!" I reported. Trampolines help with lots of things, especially boredom. And apart from my nemesis 777,777, boredom was the main enemy of OPERATION MILLION.

Obviously I wanted it. I had always wanted a trampoline. Mum and Dad said no when I had asked before, because our garden wasn't very big and it would take up too much space. Fortunately they were being helpful with my project, and they agreed that it might help with the boredom. Secretly, I expect they wanted to go on it too. Mum was also bored of lockdown. I bet she was planning to bounce on it once I had gone to bed.

Toby took the legs and the safety net off his trampoline, and made a pile of poles. Then he and his mum took out one of the fence panels between our gardens, and they carried the main bouncy part through in one go. Toby put the legs and the net back on, put the fence panel back, and there it was. I had a trampoline.

I also had some new fans. The next-door neighbours were now big supporters of OPERATION MILLION. And more were on their way.

22

If you told everyone you were going to count half a million, and then you did, it would be amazing. If you told everyone you were going to count to a million and you only got to 500,000, nobody would be impressed.

"That's only halfway," they would say.

I know this because when I got halfway, I stopped. And that's what people said. Grandad said it. Toby said it. And Toby's mum.

Not everyone said it.

"Don't be daft," is what Felix said.

• • ★ • •

By that time I had got a phone number

for Felix. Mum sorted it out. She talked to James the Half-Friend's mum and realised that she knew Felix's mum. I have discovered that when mums talk to other mums, basically anything in the world can be organised.

If people want to land on Mars for the first time, they should probably ask mums to organise it. It would be quicker than leaving it to NASA, and the guy with all the electric cars. Most of what the government does could be done better by a bunch of mums who just phone each other. The floppy-haired Prime Minister had better watch out, because one day everyone will realise this and then he won't have a job any more.

Anyway, it was great to be able to talk to Felix again. I video-called him a couple of times a week. Sometimes we did the lesson hour together. Then I got Alex's number from Felix, and Team X was back in action.

We worked out all kinds of games we could

play together online. There was one game that needed four players and we tried to call Amara, but her family only had one computer and her older brother needed it for his classes, so we didn't get to see her until school started again properly.

We mainly did quizzes and board games, sometimes even outside games on-screen. Mum said it was great to see me playing with my friends again – mostly.

She did lose it a couple of times. Alex had a trampoline too, so we decided to call each other and bounce together. I balanced Mum's laptop on the non-bouncy soft edge of the trampoline so I could see Alex. Mum nearly exploded when she saw it. Even though I hadn't accidentally jumped on the laptop yet and wasn't going to. And the laptop was only barely bouncing. I hadn't put it on the super-bouncy main part of the trampoline or anything.

There was also the time when Felix and I

thought we would play football together. If I kicked the ball against the wall and pretended the wall was Felix, he would kick his football against a wall that was me and it would be like we were kicking it to each other. To help me pretend that the wall was Felix, I called him on Mum's phone and then balanced it on the window sill so that I could see him. I was very carefully kicking the ball under the phone, not at it. But I probably don't need to tell you what Mum said about that.

After that it was mainly board games and quizzes.

Even so, that was a good reason to stop counting. Now that I had my friends back, at least a little bit, I wasn't so lonely. When I wasn't lonely, I didn't think about all the things I was missing, and the people I was missing. I didn't need the count to distract me.

School had also got more organised since the shutdown started. Before it was just lesson

169

sheets on the website. Now they were starting to do proper online lessons, one or two a week at first. You could see everyone on the screen together, and there was a "hands up" button to press to ask questions. I didn't want to miss the online lessons if my friends were there.

Besides, part of the reason I had started counting was because I was bored. Now I was bored of counting, so it was only fair to stop. So when I got to 500,000 we had a little party with lemonade and Dad, Grandad and Felix on the video call at once.

(That sentence is not very clear. I mean Dad, Grandad and Felix were on the call. The lemonade was not on the call. That was in a cup. For drinking.)

With everyone there, I counted the last few numbers up to half a million, and then everyone cheered. Grandad raised his cup of tea and said "toast", forgetting that he was on a video call and he'd have to make his own toast. Then I realised it was *a toast*, and Mum and I raised our lemonade and clinked our glasses. Grandad started to sing "For he's a jolly good fellow", but it made him go all croaky and he muted the sound on his screen while he coughed for a moment. Dad finished the song for him and then shouted, "Speech! Speech!"

"Five hundred thousand," I said. "Phew. I think I'll stop there."

Grandad unmuted himself and said, "You're only halfway!" And Felix said, "Don't be daft!"

· ● ★ ● ·

I did stop there. I didn't count for the rest of the day. When I woke up in the morning, I read my running total and it looked lovely: all those happy round zeros. Let's leave that total exactly where it is, I thought. I went downstairs and played Minecraft, and hit zombies with my diamond sword and didn't even count how many I slayed.

Of course, you will have noticed that this book

is not called *Max Counts to (half) a Million*.

There might be another book called that, by somebody else. I reckon it would be exactly half as good as this one.

Obviously, I did get to a million.

In the end.

It just took a little bit extra to get the second half done. I counted the first half for myself, and the second half for other people. Quite a lot of other people – some that I knew, and some that I didn't.

And one of those people was Grandad.

23

It was later that day that I found out. I was on the trampoline and Mum was reading on the patio. Her phone rang and she said hello in the way that meant it was Dad. Then she jumped up suddenly and she covered her mouth with her hand. She hurried inside the house and I knew straightaway that it was bad news. All the bounce seemed to go out of the trampoline. A minute later she came back, looking upset. Dad was on speakerphone.

"Are you there, Max?" he asked. He sounded serious.

"I'm here."

"I need to tell you some news. You know how Grandad's not been very well…"

"The cold he has is not a cold?" I blurted out.

A lot of people thought they had a cold at first. That's how it starts. It made me very suspicious of sneezing. Once I sneezed in the kitchen because I opened Mum's spice cupboard and breathed too hard while getting her the paprika. Even though I knew it was the spice making me sneeze, I still thought "I've got the corona!" for half a second.

So when Grandad said he had "the sniffles", obviously I guessed that maybe it wasn't.

"Yes, he took a test," said Dad. "I'm afraid he's got the virus."

I sat down and the trampoline sagged underneath me.

"How did that happen?" I asked. "There's supposed to be a shutdown going on!"

"He's been walking his friend's dog while she's

recovering from a hip operation. He thinks he got it while picking up or dropping off the dog. His friend got sick a couple of days ago."

"But he's going to be OK?" I asked quietly.

Dad hesitated in a way that made me nervous.

"I'm afraid we can't be sure about that. But Grandad is in good shape. You know how much he loves to walk. He eats a healthy diet and—"

"Well..." Mum began, and then she stopped herself. Because she's a nutritionist, Mum's idea of a healthy diet is more strict than Dad's.

"Healthier than most," said Dad. Mum did a sort of sideways nod that I think means "maybe".

"The point is that he's healthy for his age. The virus is most dangerous for people who are already unwell."

"Is he going to go to hospital?" I asked. "Then you could look after him with your doctor skills."

"It doesn't quite work like that," Dad said uncertainly. "If it's a mild case he won't need to go to hospital anyway."

"Can Grandad come and stay with us instead?"

"Not while he's infectious, no. There might be a time when we can do that, but not while I'm at the hospital and he's not well."

Dad talked some more. Mum talked some more. At some point I didn't hear them because there was a question roaring inside me. I didn't want to ask it, but it wanted to be asked.

"Dad, Grandad's not going to die, is he?"

"Oh Max, we're a long way from that," said Dad. "Please don't think that. Grandad has every chance in the world."

I nodded, but I felt the whoosh again. I hadn't felt it for a little while, but it was back. All the little jets turning on in the dark. Because Dad had not said no.

Dad finished the call because he had to go back to work. Mum asked if I was OK and I was pretty sure I was not.

"I know you don't want me to worry," I told

176

her, "but I'm scared about Grandad."

"It's perfectly normal to worry about the people you love," she replied. She came over and gave me a hug. It was a bit of a wonky one because I was still sitting on the trampoline. "It's what you do with the worry that counts."

She sighed. "You don't have to carry it all by yourself. When you tell someone your worries, you carry them together. And you can always tell me about anything that's worrying you."

Mum said it would be good to do something positive for Grandad, so we went back inside and I made a card. I drew Grandad working on the double-decker bus, like he did when he was fifteen and not old enough to be working if you ask me.

I drew it really neatly and coloured it in red. Buses don't have them today, but in the old days there was a platform on the back and you could just run and jump on. That's where Grandad would stand, and I drew him holding on to a pole

and leaning out. I added a musical note to show that he was whistling. In his hand was the clicker he had given to me on my birthday. Tiny letters on the clicker said *72*, because Grandad had told me his bus could carry seventy-two people. I would have drawn that many passengers, but there weren't enough windows to add all of them in.

"That's lovely," said Mum, and this time, unlike the not-as-good-second-rainbow incident, I agreed with her. It was fantastic. It might have been my best ever art.

"Can we go and give it to him?" I asked, forgetting about the shutdown for a moment. Grandad's house was about half an hour away in the car. You were allowed to go out to care for people, but the Prime Minister didn't want anyone driving around without a good reason. He'd been very clear on that and banged the desk about it.

"We can still catch the postman," Mum said.

When adults say this it doesn't mean actually catching the postie. Like with a trap or anything. It means you put your letter in the postbox before they get there. This is less interesting than what you might be thinking, but better for the postie.

Mum found a first-class stamp so that the card would arrive the next day, and we walked down the street to the postbox. Then I had my tea, and did a jigsaw. It had two hundred and fifty pieces and I thought about counting them, but matching up the edges was distracting enough from all the things buzzing in my head. When I felt scared about Grandad I thought about the card, and how it would make him feel better.

But there was more news.

Just as I was finishing the jigsaw, Mum's phone rang. It was Grandad's neighbour. She had cooked dinner for him and left it on the doorstep. Later she'd noticed that he hadn't come to get it. She called him to see if he was

OK, and he said he was too dizzy to go to the door.

Next she called the ambulance. It was a long wait until it arrived, but it did.

And now Grandad was in hospital.

· ∘ ★ ∘ ·

I lay in bed awake for a long time. Mum sat with me for a while. I knew she wanted to talk to Dad, so I pretended to be asleep so that she could go.

I thought about Grandad. I imagined Dad meeting the ambulance and taking Grandad up in the lift, tucking him into a comfy bed. Dad said it didn't work like that, and the hospital has different wards and he might not be on shift. But that was how I imagined it anyway.

I thought about the postie carrying my card down Grandad's street. Walking up to Grandad's front door, pushing it through the letterbox. I imagined the envelope with its first-class stamp falling on to Grandad's stripy doormat. In

Grandad's empty house.

Grandad wasn't there to get it.

What if he never got it? What if he never came home?

24

The next morning was beautiful and sunny as if nothing was wrong in the world. I tiptoed downstairs to watch some TV while I waited for Mum to wake up, but I couldn't find anything I wanted to watch. I couldn't read either. My eyes didn't want to, and I kept reading the same sentence again and again.

I wasn't sure what to do. I felt all full inside, like when you fill a cup too close to the top. Just a tiny bump and the tears would spill out.

Maybe I'd be better off counting. Maybe I should restart OPERATION MILLION after all. Except that I couldn't.

My mind didn't want to make numbers either. It was too full of tired and sadness and Grandad.

After breakfast I unlocked the back door and went out into the garden. It seemed a bit early for him to be out, but there was Toby. He was doing press-ups in the empty space where his trampoline used to be. He was counting, funnily enough. He got to thirty-seven and flopped on to the ground.

"Thirty-seven," he panted. "I hate push-ups. But I'm going to get to fifty in a row by the end of lockdown. Or die trying!"

That was even more odd than owning a trampoline that you only lie on. Why would you die trying to do something that you hate? Save your die-tryings for something you really like, I say.

"Aren't you up a bit early?" I asked.

"I'm trying to keep to a routine. Get up. Exercise. Set myself some targets – like you and your counting. How's that going, by the way?"

I told him I had stopped at 500,000. That's when he said, "That's only halfway."

I understood his disappointment. I was secretly a little disappointed with myself too, to be honest.

What's half of a millionaire?

An onaire.

That is not a real thing.

So I told Toby that I had run out of steam. And that maybe it isn't possible to count to a million anyway. And also my grandad was in hospital with Covid and I didn't feel like it any more.

Saying that out loud was like bumping the full cup, and I ran inside because I didn't want Toby to see me cry.

This time I went straight to Mum, who was sitting in bed and reading on her phone. She looked at my face and patted the space next to her. She didn't need to say anything. I didn't need to say anything either. I only cried a little bit. Mum might have cried a tiny bit too, but it was OK.

· · ★ · ·

I saw the neighbours again an hour later. I was bouncing on the trampoline quietly, and Toby's mum came out and called me over to the fence. She had a plate in her hands, covered with a tea towel.

"I made brunch for you and your mum," she said.

She handed the plate over to me and I carefully peeked under the towel. There was a stack of waffles underneath, still steaming.

"I don't know if your mum approves of waffles," said Toby's mum. "But tell her I made them with wholemeal flour."

"I think Mum will approve," said Mum, appearing suddenly from behind me and smiling. Which was a relief, because my garden isn't big enough to have a secret waffle-eating hiding place. Except maybe under the

trampoline, where spiders live.

When you see pictures of waffles in the cafe in town, they have ice cream and marshmallows and chocolate sauce on. This is not how my waffles were. It is a Nutritionist Rule that you should try and get fruit or vegetables into everything. Even using stealth. I once saw Mum make Dad an "apple and kiwi" smoothie and stick spinach in it when he wasn't looking. That's like ninja-level nutrition.

My waffles were with banana and blueberries. Some yoghurt on top, and then a tiny drizzle of honey. They still looked amazing. They tasted amazing. They would have been even more amazing with chocolate sauce. But when I lifted up the banana slices with my fork, at least there was no spinach hidden underneath. I'd call that a win.

· · ★ · ·

Mum sent me next door to give the neighbours' plate back. I put the plate on the doorstep, rang the bell and then stood back. That was the socially-distance way to do deliveries. It was Toby who answered the door.

"Aha, Max," he said.

I felt a bit embarrassed because I had run off earlier and he might have seen why. So I told him about the plate quickly so that I could go. But he said thank you and then didn't pick it up. He crossed one leg over the other and leaned on the doorpost as if he wanted to talk.

"I've been thinking about your count," he said.

I crossed one leg over the other and leaned on the wheelie bin.

"You know I was doing push-ups earlier?" asked Toby.

"You got to thirty-seven and then you nearly died," I said.

"Correct, and tomorrow maybe I'll get to thirty-eight before I nearly die. And then thirty-nine. And maybe one day I'll get to fifty. And

if I can do fifty push-ups before the end of lockdown, Mum says she'll give me a hundred pounds."

"That's good," I said.

"It is. But if you count all the way to a million, it's yours."

I nearly fell over then, because I had leaned too hard on the wheelie bin and it moved. And also because Toby wanted to give me a hundred pounds.

"You already gave me your trampoline," I reminded him.

"That's for you to keep. I was thinking the hundred pounds could be for charity. Counting to a million is pretty special, Max. I think a lot of other people would agree, and I bet they'd give money too."

"I'll prove it," he added, and leaned into the house and shouted, "Mum, if Max counts to a million, will you give him a hundred pounds?"

I didn't hear her answer, but Toby turned

back to me and said, "She says yes. So that's two hundred pounds for charity straight up. Keep going like that and you could be the new Captain Tom."

I'd heard of him. On the news I had seen stories of people doing all kinds of things to raise money for charity. A man called Captain Tom Moore, who was about a hundred and fifty years old, had walked up and down his garden. Another man had climbed the same height as Mount Everest by going up and down the stairs. There were people dressed as superheroes who were going round with collection buckets and visiting children. Could I turn my count into something like that?

"Maybe," I said to Toby. "I'm not a captain though."

"Sure you are," Toby replied. "You're the captain of OPERATION MILLION. Anyway, have a think about it and let me know if there's a charity you want to support. People are going to love it. You could help a lot of people too."

Then he picked up the plate, and I said I'd better go.

"One other thing," Toby called as I walked back to my front door. "When I said 'that's only halfway' earlier. What I meant was 'that's already halfway'."

25

I did think about Toby's idea. When I first started counting it had been to annoy Mum, which was definitely a bad thing. Then I kept going to help me not be worried and bored, which was an OK thing. What if it needed to turn into a good thing to get all the way to the end? Only the power of an excellent thing could get past the dreaded sevens.

But before I could count to a million, I needed to be able to count to 500,001.

And I still couldn't do it. I got a few numbers further. Not very far. I couldn't focus and I lost count. Every time I tried, I'd get ten or fifteen numbers in and then my mind would drift back to Grandad. Quick as a flash, all those terrible questions would come back. Was he going to be OK? What if I never saw him again?

How could I possibly count with those kinds of questions in my brain?

Mum must have had questions like that in her brain too. It made her even more quiet than usual. Bits of news arrived through the day though. Dad had found out which ward Grandad was on, and a nurse was sending him updates. He was OK. He was breathing fine. The dizziness was passing. Finally Dad got to see him, and he told us Grandad was there "for observation".

I didn't know what that meant, and Dad explained that it was good news. Grandad didn't need treatment for the virus. He was in hospital in case he did. If the sickness suddenly got worse, everything he needed would be right there.

"So Grandad is staying in hospital in case he needs to be in hospital?"

"Yes."

"Isn't that a bit like people buying all the toilet paper in case the supermarkets run out of toilet paper?" I asked. "Because we know how that ends."

"Yes we do."

"It ends with Marmite pancakes."

"Does it?" said Dad.

The next morning brought the news we had been waiting for. After two nights in hospital, Grandad had been sent home. He texted to say they were kicking him out because someone else needed his bed, otherwise he'd have stayed for the free food.

I guessed this was a joke. It's hard to tell with Grandad's texts. In real life I can look at his eyes. His eyebrows go up a tiny bit when he's joking. In a text you never know. And he does

really like free food.

The important thing was that he was out of hospital. As Mum said, that also meant he was out of danger. It might take a while for him to get back his strength, but he would get better. Then she said something that surprised me. "Shall we go and see him?"

We all knew that wasn't allowed, not really.

"Just this once," said Mum. "We'll stay outside so there's no contact. We'll just leave him some supplies outside the door. It's a care trip."

I was pretty sure the Prime Minister wouldn't like it, but we went to the shop anyway.

There was a queue at the shop because only a few people were allowed in at a time. Mum put her mask on, which was important to stop the tiny zombies parachuting into your face. I wore one too, because it made me feel like a bandit.

Except that bandits don't queue. They just run in and shout "Hands up!" and "Hand over all the crisps and biscuits and nobody gets hurt."

194

Or the money. I think in real life bandits are mainly interested in money.

We bought things for Grandad. I thought we were getting treats to make him feel better. Mum saw it differently. "We need to make sure he doesn't end up eating junk while he's too tired to cook properly." So Mum chose something and then I chose something, that was the deal. Mum got some vitamin pills for Grandad, and I got him a bar of chocolate. Mum got a bag of mixed nuts and seeds, and I got him some broccoli.

"Wait a second," said Mum. "Broccoli? Who is this child, and what have you done with Max?"

"It is supposed to be good for you," I replied. "And now is the perfect time for Grandad to eat lots of it, while he can't taste anything."

We parked the car outside Grandad's house. Then Mum carried all the treats and the useful boring things over to the front door and put

the bag down on the doorstep. She rang the doorbell and then came back to me, standing a long way from the house, next to the car.

There was quite a long wait. I began to wonder if Grandad was there.

Finally the door opened and I saw Grandad. He looked pale and was moving slowly. I noticed that he had a scarf on even though it wasn't winter. He looked down and saw the bag. Then he looked up and saw us. I did a happy jump inside when he smiled. That would have been a good time for a hug, but seeing him would have to be enough.

Standing on the pavement with the front garden between us, we couldn't really talk to Grandad. Instead, he held up his finger in a "wait there" kind of a way. Then he took the shopping inside, and a minute later Mum's phone rang. I could just hear Grandad's voice from the phone and it was all deep and whispery.

"You shouldn't have come all this way for me,"

said Grandad, appearing in the living-room window and giving me a wave.

"Well, we were worried about you. And Max wanted to see you."

"And I wanted to see Max," said Grandad. "Thank you."

Then he held something up to the window. It was my card with the picture of the bus.

It had made it to Grandad. Grandad had made it home.

· · ★ · ·

We couldn't talk for long because it made Grandad cough. And we couldn't stand around for too long in the street in case the police or the Prime Minister came along. So we waved goodbye and drove home.

I still felt full to the brim somehow, but it wasn't with sadness. It was with something else. I didn't know what to call it, but I felt like Grandad was going to be OK. Even though he didn't look well yet, I felt like everything was going to be all right. And that I could do anything, and that anything was going to include counting to a million.

Before I knew it, I was counting the cars.

There weren't many cars about, so I started counting streetlights instead. I rolled them into my big count. There still weren't enough, so I switched to counting the houses. I said the numbers out loud as we flashed by in the car, and I saw Mum smile at me in the rear-view mirror.

When we arrived home, I saw that somebody had tied a big banner to our fence along the driveway. It read *OPERATION MILLION*. There was a sign leaning on the wheelie bin, saying *You can do it!*

26

Adults often ask children what they want to be when they grow up. I think it's something that adults ask when they don't know what else to say.

The truth is, I have no idea what I will be when I grow up. It's too soon to tell.

There is one thing I definitely won't be, and that is someone who counts things for their job. I think that's called an accountant, but I might be wrong. They mainly count money and stuff. Now that I've counted to a million, I could probably call myself an accountant if I wanted to. I've got the experience.

Well, there is one thing I'm missing.

You have to wear a tie if you're an accountant, and a proper one too. Mine from school is only a clip-on, which would not be good enough in a professional office. Nobody would trust me to count their money with a clip-on tie. So I'd need to learn to tie a tie, but basically apart from that I could be an accountant.

If I wanted to be. And I do not.

For one thing, I had to wear a real tie for a wedding once and it was a total faff.

Mainly, I never want to count anything ever again.

I plan to count one thing a year for the rest of my life. Every year, on my birthday, I will count one extra year to make sure I have enough candles on my cake. Otherwise, I won't count anything.

The second half of the million was different from the first. For a start, I had a mission.

I talked to Mum and Dad about Toby's idea.

Dad said that there was a charity that was raising money to help the NHS during the pandemic. They were the same charity that Captain Tom Moore was raising money for and they were called NHS Charities Together. They were helping NHS staff and patients too.

"We were lucky that I was able to see Grandad, but imagine being in hospital and not being able to have visitors," Dad said. "NHS Charities Together have been sending us equipment so that we can set up virtual visits. I've seen the difference that makes to people who are on the wards and who are feeling so alone."

We were sitting at the table outside, Dad on the video link. It was another beautiful clear blue sky. I looked up to see if the swifts were there. They were, so high up you'd only notice them if you looked hard. The first bird members of my team, even though they didn't have an X in their name.

"Everybody needs to have a team around

them," I said.

"Yes they do, Max," Dad replied.

· · ★ · ·

Another big difference with the second half of the count was that other people were involved. I had been counting all by myself, and nobody really knew about it. Now the news was getting around. On Thursdays we clapped for the NHS, and then Mr Gupta across the street would shout, "How many, Max?" or "Update?" Then I would shout out my total, and everybody would clap for me. Then the adults would stand around talking. Someone would ask about Grandad, and we would tell them any news. They would ask if anybody needed anything. Toby's mum said that she'd been to see old Mrs Jessup down the road, because her husband had been in hospital.

I noticed that Ava who lives on my street was coming down from her house to clap nearer to ours. She lives about ten doors down, and every week she seemed to be one house closer. Before long she'd be next door, then on the driveway, and within three weeks she'd be climbing in the window and clapping in our living room.

There were banners too. The big one with OPERATION MILLION on it, and then cardboard signs that friends from school had made. "All the way", "You can do it", "To the Max". At least two said "Maxey Million" or some version of Maximillian, which isn't my name, and I did not approve of these. One had a big red heart on it and "1,000,000 xs", which seemed to suggest a million kisses. I wondered if that was from Ava.

Soon OPERATION MILLION was on the Internet. Mum had set up a fundraising page so people could make donations. Mum and Dad shared it with their friends, then those friends sent it to their friends, and then it got bigger and bigger.

Then Mum set up a meeting with NHS Charities Together. Apart from school, I'd

never been to a meeting before. Certainly not one where everyone wanted to talk about my project, and where grown-ups kept asking, "What do you think, Max?" all the time as if I was the boss.

After lots of talking, we decided that any money that people gave to OPERATION MILLION would pay for something called "befriending schemes".

"Befriending is for people who are lonely," said Mum, noticing that I hadn't understood. "For people who are isolating and don't have anyone to talk to or check that they're okay." I guessed that the volunteers they were training were people then, and not bees. But I still spent the next few minutes not paying attention to the meeting and wondering what it would be like to have a little bee as a friend.

The people from the charity were very excited about all of this, and they made a banner to go outside the house. It said "Max Counts to a

Million" at the top, and then "for NHS Charities Together" underneath. Then there was a blank white space where Mum wrote the total amount of money that had been raised so far. We tied it up at the front of the house and Mum took a picture of me standing in front of it.

That was the picture that went in the local newspaper, in the first article about me.

After that, people started beeping their car horns when they drove past the house.

With the banners and the story in the local paper, donations started to come in faster and faster. During the first day the total went from £200 to £2,000. By the end of the week it had got to £10,000. In the mornings Mum checked the fundraising page and then went out and updated the total on the banner at the front of the house.

Adults get quite excited about big amounts of money, but it was just a number. It would

have been more exciting if there was an actual big pile of money on the driveway, and people walked past and threw more of it into the pile. That would have been more real than a number on a banner.

Obviously that couldn't be paper money, if it was all in a pile at the front. It would blow away or get wet in the rain. It would need to be coins, which are the best kind of money. That would have been excellent, if the whole driveway was just knee-deep in coins. Hopefully two-pound coins, because those are my favourite. Maybe there could be treasure chests to keep things neat.

Mum said a lot of people weren't using cash so much these days because of the pandemic. They were afraid the coins would have the virus on them. Fair enough. I wouldn't mind if those people wanted to chuck gold or diamonds on to the pile instead, that would also be fine. You can probably buy things with diamonds if you go to the right kind of shop.

If you were doing it that way, you would need a guard or the police there. Otherwise people might come by and steal money instead of giving it, and that would be pointless.

None of that happened though. The charity wanted to do it all online, which is much more boring but definitely easier.

· · ★ · ·

Everyone at school had found out about the count by now. Felix and Alex agreed that OPERATION MILLION was a Team X project and not just mine any more. They made some posters and then on their daily walks they delivered them to everyone's house in the class.

Then Amara organised The Pirates to deliver posters to the other two classes in our year. Soon I saw posters saying "Go Max!" in people's front windows all around the area, along with the NHS rainbow pictures. I knew that loads of families were cheering for me. It was also good

to know that we could depend on our alliance with The Pirates.

The school helped too. They put an article on their website, and started putting the fundraising total on their Facebook page each day. The article made it very clear that I was still doing lessons, just in case any other children decided that they could stop doing schoolwork and just count.

They also sent Miss Jenkins round to check on my learning, and we had a meeting on the driveway. I've never been sure about Miss Jenkins. It's the trouser leg tucked into the sock thing.

But she arrived on her bike, and I realised that she tucks her trouser leg up like that so it doesn't go in the bike chain. That's actually quite sensible. Miss Jenkins is not weird after all, just forgetful. If she'd remembered to untuck the flappy leg of her trousers when she parked her bike, I wouldn't have spent half the year thinking she was odd.

Anyway, Miss Jenkins said that the school wanted to support one of their children in an ambitious project. They could see the educational value of OPERATION MILLION, and that it was character-building. The main problem was that I might fall behind in my English if I only counted for two whole months.

To make up for it, Miss Jenkins gave me a book of writing exercises and word puzzles to work through when I was done with the count. She also suggested that maybe I could do a writing project of some kind when I was finished. Even if it went into the summer holidays.

"Deal?" she said.

"Deal," I said.

As we all know, a deal isn't official unless you shake hands, and that wasn't allowed with the social distancing. So we did an "air" handshake across two metres, and Miss Jenkins laughed.

I laughed too. An air handshake is a funny

thing to do, especially with a teacher. I was also laughing for another reason: if Miss Jenkins forgets to untuck her trousers from her socks, there was a good chance she would forget all about my summer writing project.

27

There was a problem with all this attention though. The best way to count to a million is just to keep going and not be interrupted. The more people knew about the count, the more interruptions there were. Everyone wanted updates on how far I had got to. The local radio station wanted an interview. NHS Charities Together had lots of ideas involving people counting with me. A photographer came and knocked on the door.

I didn't mind most of this. I love talking to people and, to be honest, I'm also a bit of a show-off. But my counting had slowed down with too many people bothering me.

Mum basically started working on OPERATION MILLION. She called herself my agent. She answered the phone and the door, and told me about things later. Some of her work was restarting, but she still had plenty of time to help. She sat at the dining table and replied to emails about the count, and sent thank-you messages to people who were giving money. It turns out that there was a lot more to the project than just counting, and it was great to work together with Mum to get all those other non-counting jobs done.

I did an interview with the radio. It didn't go very well. I was annoyed because the very first thing the presenter said was, "Heyyy, Maximillian!" and I had to correct him.

We talked about how far I had got, and then about the fundraising. I had practised what to say about the charity and befriending, to make sure I got it right. Then the radio guy said, "I bet you're really good at counting to twenty while you're washing your hands!"

I knew about this of course, because that was a thing that people did. You were supposed to count to twenty or sing a song to make sure you washed your hands for long enough.

"No, I don't count to twenty."

"More of a song person then," said the DJ, butting in. "So what's your song of choice?"

"It's one by a band that my mum likes."

"Oh, OK. Have you've changed the words?"

"I changed the words in the chorus so it goes 'This is what you get, coronavirus, tiny zombie scum'."

The DJ hummed it and said, "Yes, I see how that works. But wait a minute – tiny zombie scum?"

"Because viruses aren't really alive or dead, like zombies," I explained, but the radio man

just laughed.

"My dad is a doctor, so I know quite a lot about it," I reminded him.

Then he just said, "Maximillian everybody, and best of luck to him as the count goes on," and played another song without even saying goodbye.

Clearly you don't need to get people's names right to be a radio DJ. Or be polite. Or understand science.

After that I tried not to do too many interviews. I did updates a couple of times a day instead, and Mum filmed me with her phone and then put the videos on the fundraising page. But when the TV news called, Mum said that would be good to do. They phoned in the morning, and were going to come round after lunch. Mum made me wash my face and put on a smarter shirt.

I had been wearing my Batman T-shirt with a

cape that attaches to the back with Velcro. I got it for my seventh birthday and I was too big for it really, but it looks great when I bounce on the trampoline. Mum didn't agree. "You don't want to be wearing a cape on television," she said, even though TV is the main place that you see people in capes.

I was just counting some tiny poppy seeds on my plate (nutritionists love bread with tiny seeds on it) when the TV van arrived outside. It parked by the driveway and I went over to the living-room window to have a look. Then I nearly fell over backwards off the sofa, because the door of the van opened, and out stepped Bea Hixby.

In real life.

On my driveway.

She saw me in the window and waved, and I nearly fell off the sofa again.

Mum opened the door and straightaway I said, "Hello, Bea Hixby." Mum seemed surprised that I knew who she was already, but she doesn't

know about Team X.

"Nice to meet you, Max. You can call me Bea."

Of course I could call her Bea. I don't know why I always thought of her as Bea Hixby, all in one name.

Bea had a cameraman with her, called Alan. They set up the camera on the driveway, making sure you could see the banners in the background. A car came by and beeped loudly.

"Oh, that must get annoying," said Bea, and Mum agreed. I quite like the beeping myself. I imagined that every beep was a pound going into the fundraiser, which had now gone up to £28,000.

Bea held a microphone on a long stick and did an interview with Mum. Mum talked about the charity, and also about Dad and Grandad and how lockdown had been difficult at times. That was the serious bit. Then I did an interview and I got more fun questions, like how I didn't get bored, and all the different ways I'd found to count.

"I hear you've been asking for food that can be counted," said Bea. "What's the best food for counting to a million?"

"Rice," I replied. "I tried couscous but it was too small and fiddly. Pasta is a bit too big. With rice you get about a thousand of them on a plate and that's perfect."

"Excellent," said Bea with a smile. She really did have a nice face. Even nicer in real life. "And what are you going to eat to celebrate getting to a million?"

"A jacket potato. Then if I'm tempted to start counting, I'll only get to one and I can stop and enjoy my food."

The cameraman wanted to film me counting, but nobody was allowed into the house during shutdown. One person in the garden was OK, so I showed Bea the way around the side of the house and in the back gate at the end of the garden. She filmed me counting on the

stepping stones, and lying on my back looking at the clouds and clicking Grandad's tally counter. I counted and kicked the football on the wall, and then on the trampoline. I showed her my running total, with all the crossed-out totals before it, going back on pages and pages of my notebook.

All of this was called "footage" for some reason. "Let's get some footage of you counting on your fingers," she'd say. Or, "We've got some really good footage here." (I have looked this up to see why footage is called that. The answer is educational if you are in the mood for some education later.)

When Bea had done enough filming she put the camera down carefully on the table in the garden. "Before we go," she said, "I am totally going on your trampoline."

Mum had been watching, and Bea turned to her and said, "That's OK, isn't it?" And when Mum nodded, Bea added, "Do you mind telling

Alan I'll be another five minutes?"

Then it was just the two of us in the garden, with Bea Hixby on the trampoline.

This was possibly the best day of my life.

I would have bounced with her if it hadn't been for social distancing. That would have been awesome. Instead I sat on the edge of the frame while she bounced, and her brown hair flew up around her nice face.

"Bea, can I ask you a question?" I asked. Which is itself a question, in fact. So I already had.

"Of course. I've been asking you all the questions so far, so that's only fair."

"I've noticed that you're not on the news every day. What are you doing on the other days?"

"Oh, you know – other assignments. Helping out on other stories." And then she laughed and said, "Secret missions."

"I thought so," I said. "You know, we're on the same team, you and me. Because we both have

219

an X in our name."

"That's right," said Bea. "Although I actually have two. Not many people know this, but Bea is short for Beatrix."

Mum came back into the garden then and it was time for the TV crew to go, so I didn't get to ask any more questions. But as I watched them drive away, I smiled to myself.

Beatrix Hixby.

Two Xs. It had been her all along.

Double X.

28

Being on the TV news was good for OPERATION MILLION. *Very* good.

We watched the news report in the evening. Dad had it on the TV in his hotel room and joined us on a video call. So did Grandad. He had been feeling very tired and spent a lot of time in bed. We sent each other messages every day, but we hadn't had a call and so it was special to see him on the screen again. Maybe knowing I was on the news had given him a burst of energy. Or maybe he had eaten all the broccoli.

We were at the end of the news. "And finally, the boy who has been spending the lockdown counting to a million. And he's not far off either. Our community reporter Bea Hixby went to meet him."

And then there I was on TV, bouncing on the trampoline and counting loudly. 682,327. 682,328. "Meet Max Cromwell," said Bea's voice. "A nine-year-old on a mission."

Then there was stuff with Mum, and some questions with me on the driveway. They left in a car beeping and spoiling it a bit, because it showed how the community was supporting me. The report included a bit from one of my video updates that Mum had filmed, and some footage of befriending volunteers phoning people. It ended with me back on my trampoline and Bea's voice saying, "We'll be back when Max hits his big target. Until then, keep going Max – we're counting on you!"

"You're a rock star, Max!" said Grandad from Mum's laptop.

"You're a natural," added Dad.

"Max was very relaxed and confident with the reporter," said Mum.

"Well, Bea is a friend of mine."

While I was talking about the filming with Dad and Grandad, Mum got her phone and went on to the fundraising page. She gasped and said, "Max!" We all looked at her. "You've raised fifty thousand pounds!"

She spoke too soon, because five minutes later it was sixty thousand, and then seventy. It was the news viewers. Thanks to Bea's good reporting and my interview skills, loads of people were hurrying over to the fundraising page.

By the time Mum finally sent me to bed, the total had shot past a quarter of a million pounds.

· · ★ · ·

I thought that there was only one TV news. Apparently not. There are lots of different news programmes. I don't know why this is necessary. The news is the news.

There are whole channels of news. Just the

news, all day. It sounds boring, but I suppose it's for people who want to know what's happening right now, and can't wait until the evening.

I learned this because the next day there were phone calls and interruptions all day. For Mum, at least. I powered through some Minecraft-block counting, some trampoline, my usual musical section. I did some counting that came with a little dance, and a punch in the air every time I got past a ten. There was still a long way to go, and I ignored everything else that was going on.

Over lunch, Mum asked if I wanted to do something called a "press briefing".

"You're in high demand," she said. "You can say no if you want to."

I looked at the living-room window and noticed that the curtains were closed.

"Yes, there are quite a few cameras out there," Mum confirmed.

Mum explained that a press briefing was

when you talked to lots of reporters at once to save time. Sometimes you said a few things that you wanted to say, and then they could ask questions. I realised that this is what they had on the news every evening, when people asked the politicians about the coronavirus. They always stood behind a little desk that said "Stay home > Protect the NHS > Save lives".

"Should I stand behind a little desk?" I asked.

"If you like," said Mum.

Then she made me a sign, with yellow and red edges like the government's ones. It said:

Start counting > Keep going > Count to a million

We printed it, taped it to the back of a chair, and I stood behind it at 3 o'clock while people from the news asked me questions. I wore my clip-on tie.

Mum was very strict with the reporters. She made them all spread out and keep two metres apart. They all shouted at once, and they

were wearing masks, so it was all a bit muffled and confusing. Mum made them stop and ask questions one at a time. "What's your favourite number?" "How long do you think it's going to take?" "Do you think your fundraising will catch up to Captain Tom?" Then when everybody had asked one question, she sent me back inside and answered a few more.

When she came back in, she closed the front door and slumped against the wall.

"Well, don't just stand there," she said when I asked if she was all right. "Count to a million! The sooner this is over the better!"

· · ★ · ·

The next day all the papers had pictures of me standing behind my red and yellow sign. By lunchtime the fundraising total had gone past half a million. It was going to get to a million pounds before I got to a million on the count. Sure enough, by bedtime the counter had clicked past the big million.

I had made it to a million. A different million.

That got even more attention. Mum told all the news people that I wasn't doing any more press stuff or I'd never finish the count, but they kept asking. Sometimes there was a photographer waiting outside and we had to sneak out the back gate to go for our exercise. Now there were journalists from other countries calling, and Grandad started helping with interviews. He insisted that he felt strong enough, and that helping out made him feel better. That suited Mum fine, because she'd had enough of talking to reporters. She turned her phone off and spent her lunch break lying in the sun with her book.

Meanwhile, I had troubles of my own, because I had got to the dreaded sevens.

Even with my improved counting systems, the 700,000s were slow. I could feel the evil plan of Team Z to make me give up. "You'll never make it to 777,777," they seemed to say. "You always knew this is where you'd give up."

I had been counting for seven weeks. All the sevens were ganging up on me at once.

I had to find new ways to keep going. I tried to imagine that every time I counted a number, a Covid zombie died. That was fun for a while. Or I imagined that if I got to a million, it would cure the virus. Everything would go back to normal and Dad could come home. Everyone was cheering for me to do it, because only I could save the world by getting to a million.

I looked up and watched the swifts spelling M-A-X in the sky. I thought of Bea saying, "We're counting on you", and Felix saying "Don't be daft" when I said that I wanted to quit. I thought about the fundraising. I thought about doing something positive for Grandad.

But it was still difficult.

It was still boring.

I hate the number seven.

29

Lockdown went on and on. The blue skies went on and on. The counting went on and on. Every day seemed the same, week after week.

But every day was not the same. Little by little, the virus was being defeated. Not so many people were getting sick. The hospitals were not as full.

And that meant happy news: Dad could come home.

He came home on a Thursday afternoon. That was the last Thursday when people did the clapping for the NHS. When we stepped outside, there were people all up and down the street, and a whole crowd around our driveway. Everyone was being careful to keep two metres apart and stay safe, so some people were standing in the road. Which was unsafe in a different way.

Honestly, if you are trying to avoid coronavirus and get hit by a car instead, that is just an epic fail.

I think most of the crowd had come to see me, because I was quite famous by then. I put my arms around Dad and Mum, one on each side, while the clapping happened. Obviously with my arms busy doing hugs, I wasn't able to clap. So I actually didn't do the last clap for the NHS properly. But that was OK. The hugs were more important. I was so proud of my dad, and I wanted all the claps to be for him.

Even though he was excited to be home and looking forward to a few days off, Dad did not want me to stop or slow down my count – not now that I had got this far. And I was so pleased to be counting with him around that

I actually forgot all about how much I hated sevens until I counted all the way up to 777,770.

"Hey Dad," I called from the trampoline, while Dad sat with Mum on the lawn. "Come and count with me."

When he came over, I explained that sevens were longer, and so this was the longest bit of the whole count. It was like riding a bike uphill, when your legs are all sore and the hill is still going on. So we counted it out loud together.

777,771
777,772
777,773
777,774
777,775
777,776
777,777

BOOM. Take that, Team Z!

Nothing can stop me now.

I had crushed the sixfold seven, the worst

number of them all. Now I was riding downhill all the way to a million.

· ◦ ★ ◦ ·

I mean, I still had at least two weeks of counting to go. It wasn't that fast, but it was definitely different. Dad was there. He got up with me in the morning and tucked me in at night. He was there at every mealtime. I could count and kick the football to him instead of the wall. He helped Mum with the news and talking to the charity. The most important thing was that Dad was never far away.

Except during my daily musical hour. Then he was often somewhere else. Busy. I guess Dad doesn't like jazz either.

· ◦ ★ ◦ ·

One thing that Dad came up with was hosting live counting events as part of the fundraising. People could join in and count with me online – sometimes it was people from a business who wanted to give some money. Sometimes it was for TV. Sometimes it was a classroom. The most distracting ones were with children from my own school, because it was people I knew and everyone wanted to say hello. And I wanted to say hello back to them too, and then we'd never actually do any counting.

Dad was strict about how it worked so that it didn't take up too much time. He would talk to everybody and answer questions, and then carry the laptop over to me. I would wave without stopping my count. When I got to the next round number, like a 100, Dad would give everyone a countdown and they'd have to try and keep up with me.

Nobody could. I was well practised, and I didn't slow down for anybody.

I'm not trying to boast, but I might be the fastest at counting in the world right now. Nobody would keep up with me. Not even the best accountants.

· · ★ · ·

233

There was a final surprise in those last couple of weeks that helped me through to the end.

The doorbell rang one morning and Mum answered it. Mum didn't usually interrupt my counting, but this time she called for me. It was Ava. She had a present for me.

"It's a bit random," she said. "I was trying to think of ways to make your counting more fun. And this is what I came up with."

She was standing on the driveway next to two buckets, with a long bit of guttering in between them like a bridge.

"I'll show you how it works," she said. "This is some spare guttering from my dad's shed." Then she called me over and pointed to what was inside one of the buckets. "And in here is a thousand marbles that I bought from eBay."

I realised that I had never actually spoken to Ava on her own before, even though she lived on my street. And she had just bought me a thousand marbles on eBay.

"All you do is roll the marbles down, one at a time, into the other bucket." She demonstrated. "That's a thousand. Then you just change the tilt of the gutter and roll them back the other way."

I noticed that she had cut U-shaped grooves into the side of the bucket. If you put the gutter into the U on one side, it sloped in that direction.

This was actually quite clever.

Ava was actually quite clever.

I moved her up several levels on my friend scale.

"Do you want to count a thousand with me right now?" I asked, and we did, right there on the driveway. It took a while. Longer than usual, even when I had explained System 221B. But Ava had given me a thousand marbles, two buckets and a gutter. Nobody had done that before and I didn't mind slowing down a bit so she could keep up.

30

I bet you can guess what happens next. I mean, if you can't, you really haven't been paying attention. This book is called *Max Counts to a Million.*

Spoiler alert!

This is the bit where I finally get to a million.

· · ★ · ·

With all the attention that OPERATION MILLION had received, the world records people had got in touch. They said that the record for the first person to count to a million was taken by the man called Jeremy who I had read about on the Internet. He also had the record for the highest number ever counted.

If I completed my count, I'd be able to claim the youngest person ever to count to a million. He had done it in eighty-nine days, so if I did it in less time, I could also get the fastest count to a million.

Unfortunately there was a problem. In fact there were two. One was System 221B. Apparently there is some kind of records committee who have to discuss these things. We had a video call with the five of them, and they told us what the trouble was. They said that if you were counting properly, you would have to do each number in full. With my system, I was just saying the number rather than counting it. Other members of the committee said that was rubbish. They had a vote. My system passed the vote.

Another committee member said the main problem wasn't my shorter and quicker way of saying the numbers. The problem was that I had changed part way into the count. I should have chosen one system or another at the beginning, and stuck with it. There was another vote. I won that one too.

As they discussed it, another problem came up. How did they know that I had actually done it? I didn't launch the fundraiser and start telling people about it until halfway. What if I'd made it up? Maybe I'd only started at 500,000.

Obviously Mum and Dad knew I'd started at the beginning. And Grandad. But that was family, and maybe we were working together to tell a lie. Toby and the neighbours didn't know about it until almost 150,000. They seemed to be quite sorry about it, but the records committee were very clear. If I couldn't prove when I had started, they couldn't give me the records.

That was all very disappointing. I still had the fundraising, but the world records would have been the icing on the cake. We were about to end the call when Dad remembered something.

He got his phone and dialled a number.

"Hello," he said when they picked up. "This is going to sound very odd, but do you mind talking to the world records committee?" Then he put his phone on speakerphone. It was Dr Grace. She told the committee how she had seen me reach my first thousand, while she was in the hospital staffroom.

The grumpiest member of the committee still wasn't happy. "It's not proof of starting at zero though, is it?" he complained. They had another vote, and he was the only one who voted against my records.

All I had to do was get there, and for the last couple of weeks I had so many different ways to count that I hardly got bored. Rolling marbles was especially good. It made a lovely sound as they rumbled down the gutter and clicked into the pile in the bucket, and you could see exactly how many you had to go to tick off the

next thousand. So Ava is basically a genius and is now officially my friend.

When school restarted, I discovered that her full name is Ava Lennox Wharton. She was a member of Team X all along.

· · ★ · ·

On the last few days, lots and lots of news people wanted to film me reaching my target. That wasn't really possible with social distancing, but we did want to have a few guests. We decided to do it at the front of the house where people could see. Mum carefully chalked out two-metre squares so that people knew how far to stand from each other. We made a guest list.

For the last couple of days I kept a careful track of how much I was counting each day, so that I could finish exactly when I wanted to.

I finished on day sixty-three. Two whole months of counting. Dad was pretty much right.

I woke up early and counted the last few thousand, so that I only had the last thousand to do by the afternoon grand finale. Then I counted down to the last 500, and then all the way to 999,900.

One hundred to go for the million. Then I stopped and had lunch and felt nervous.

At two o'clock we opened the front door and saw everybody there.

The most important people were Felix and Alex, and Grandad, who was well enough to drive over and be there for the big moment. He sat in a garden chair in his own chalk square, next to Ava and her parents. Toby and his mum watched from their driveway, Mr and Mrs Gupta waved from across the street. Two people from NHS Charities Together were there, proudly standing next to a banner with the final fundraising total of £3,032,190. If you've read this far, you'll know that's more than three million pounds! Mrs Pine was there from school. There was one cameraman, and one photographer who would send photos to all the papers. There

was a woman from the world records committee to check it all went to plan.

There was one other very important person. Standing next to the cameraman was Bea Hixby, the only reporter at the event. Mum had invited her and she had sent back a text that said:

"Of course. Happy to support Max on his big day. Bea xx"

Anyone else would have thought that the xx at the end of the message were kisses. I knew better.

I started counting out loud.

To be honest, it was a big moment and my voice went a bit shaky. A lot of people were watching, and I was about to finish a very long and very big challenge. I could feel the whoosh in my stomach, but this time it wasn't worry, it was excitement. Mum and Dad joined in, and then Grandad, and then Felix and Ava and Alex, and soon everyone was counting together.

We got louder as we went along, until we got

to the final ten. I wasn't nervous then. Some people stopped counting so I could do it by myself, but I waved my arms to encourage them to keep going. I wanted to do it together.

999,997

999,998

999,999

ONE MILLION!

A huge cheer went up. Mum started crying. Dad did a dance that he later said was undignified. Alex and Felix jumped about. Social-distancing rules were nearly broken as people went to hug each other and remembered they weren't supposed to.

And me?

I said: "One million and one."

Bet you didn't see that coming, did you?

Twist ending!

The man who had counted to a million before had the record for the highest number ever counted out loud. All I had to do was count to a

million and one, and I would set a new record. So I set three world records on the same day.

Just to make sure, I counted to a million and nine, because I was nine.

And that's about it.

· ● ★ ● ·

Well, nearly. After all the jumping around and cheering, I did another interview with Bea. Then I helped her and the cameraman to roll up all the cables as they packed the TV camera away. People started to go home and Dad and I carried the folding chairs back into the garden. I was just coming out of the house when I noticed Grandad getting into his car on the other side of the street.

"Wait, you forgot to say goodbye!" I shouted. But Grandad did not drive away. He turned his car on to the driveway and got back out again. And he had a suitcase with him.

"I'm not going anywhere," he said. "I'm going to stay for a couple of weeks. And I know it won't be the one you expected, but I think you're owed a birthday party."

I ran and hugged him, and I hugged him for a long time.

· ○ ★ ○ ·

And that really is it.

I had a holiday, and Grandad came too. And then after all that maths, I sat down to do some English. Which I have now done.

And yes, I could have called the book *Max Counts to a Million and Nine*. But that isn't a very good title, and it definitely would be a spoiler.

Bonus quiz!

Congratulations, you have finished the book. You are allowed to stop here if you're not interested in quizzes. That's fine. Bye-bye!

If you do like quizzes, you're in luck. I've done one for you.

Quizzes is a dodgy word, isn't it? Two actual Zs, and then the "es" sound at the end is basically another Z. It's the world's most zeddy word…

Tangent, alert: Danger! Danger!

That was a close one. Don't worry, I'll get on with the quiz.

1. What is a "pandemic"?
   a) A microphone for pandas
   b) Everything going wrong in the kitchen
   c) A disease that spreads everywhere in the world
   d) A drum kit made of pots and pans

2. Which is the best letter?
   a) Y
   b) X
   c) Z
   d) A

3. Who or what is Max's nemesis?
   a) Miles
   b) The number 777,777
   c) Team Z
   d) Courgettes

4. **What does NHS stand for?**
   a) National Health Service
   b) Naughty Halloween Spook
   c) Not Healthy Snack
   d) Number Hated: Seven

5. **What is a "nutritionist"?**
   a) The person in charge of all the nuts
   b) Someone who takes away sweets
   c) An expert on healthy eating
   d) Your mum

6. **If there is ever a war or a showdown, who will be the allies of Team X?**
   a) Team Z
   b) Amara and The Pirates
   c) The Tiny Zombies
   d) Friendly bees

Answers:

1. **c**
2. **b** and if you said **c** then you basically need to read the whole book again.
3. **b** but all of those answers are acceptable on certain days.
4. **a**
5. **c** unless your mum is also a nutritionist and then it can also be **d**.
6. **b**

Author's note
Counting to a million in real life

Max is a made-up character, and this whole story is fiction. Which is a shame, because I'd rather like Max to be real. There are some true things in the book though. The coronavirus pandemic is real, of course. It's true that some key workers had to stay away from their families like Max's dad did. Putting that in a story is one way to say thank you to everyone who had to do that.

The schools did have to close. Perhaps yours did. Putting that in the story is a way of capturing that unique experience for children in the future to read about.

The amount of money that Max raised is made up, but it is true that people did all sorts of amazing things to raise money during the pandemic. NHS Charities Together is a real charity, and you've made a donation to them by buying this book!

It's also true that in 2007 a man called Jeremy Harper counted to a million. He counted in front of a webcam so anyone on the Internet could watch him the whole time. Jeremy's project was called MillionCount and it raised $12,000 for a charity for people with disabilities called Push America. He didn't leave his house for the entire time and he didn't shave, so he had a huge beard by the end, and he did do a little chicken dance when he finished!

Jeremy counted for 16 hours each day, and it took him 89 days. I made Max go faster than that by giving him the quicker way to count, but some people would consider that cheating. If you want to go for a world record, it's best to check if there are any rules first!

Finally, Jeremy Harper is in Guinness World

Records for the "highest number reached while counting aloud". So it's true that you could break his record by counting to one million and one, like Max does in the last chapter.

But don't do that. I like it when world records belong to people called Jeremy. Apart from a few annoying ones that are banned, anyone called Jeremy is automatically on my team, the Secret Union of Jeremys. (It's secret, so don't tell anyone.)

Jeremy Williams, September 2020

Acknowledgements

A big thank you to Megan Carroll for taking on a writer better known for deeply unfunny books for adults, and to Laetitia Rutherford for the introduction.

Thank you to Nosy Crow for seeing the value in the pandemic setting, and being willing to crash the schedule for Max. Thank you to Fiona Scoble and Kate Wilson for bringing more emotional depth and a broader set of characters to the story, and to Fiona for refining and focusing the book in so many ways.

Consider yourselves to be honorary members of Team X.

Thanks to all my test readers, in Luton and beyond, especially Miss Clay and

Miss Bright's classes at Wenlock Junior School.

Thank you to Lucy Marcovitch and Dr Sarah Carman.

Big thanks and much love to Lou, who holds the space for me to write, reads everything first and always makes it better. And to Zach and Eden, whose experiences of the pandemic inspired so many details, and who always laugh in the right places.